MASSIVE CLEANSING FIRE

DAVE HOUSLEY

Outpost19 | San Francisco
outpost19.com

Housley, Dave
          Massive Cleansing Fire/ Dave Housley
          ISBN 9781944853143 (pbk)

Library of Congress Control Number: pending

UNCORRECTED
REVIEW COPY

Minor corrections to the text and cover
will be incorporated before the final printing.
Thanks very much for your interest.

Pub date: 2/1/2017
Distributor: Ingram Publisher Services
For review and author info, contact
Jon Roemer jon@outpost19.com

outpost19.com
facebook.com/outpost19
@outpost19

OUTPOST19

ORIGINAL
PROVOCATIVE
READING

Also by Dave Housley

If I Knew The Way, I Would Take You Home
Commercial Fiction
Ryan Seacrest Is Famous
Four Fathers

MASSIVE CLEANSING FIRE

Every thing that may abide the fire,
ye shall make it go through the fire,
and it shall be clean.

NUMBERS 31:23

THE COMBAT PHOTOGRAPHER

The combat photographer needed health care. Not for a piece of shrapnel in the knee or a stray bullet to the shoulder, not for injuries sustained while running to the site of a car bomb, or thrombosis or malaria or even food poisoning. There was a baby on the way, and his wife was drawing the line.

"I'm sick and tired of it," the combat photographer's wife said. "Gallivanting all over the place. Sudan. Afghanistan. Iraq. It's one thing to leave me for months at a time. It's another to leave your child."

"It's what I do," the combat photographer said. "I'm a combat photographer."

The combat photographer's wife tapped her foot and folded her arms across her belly. She patted the bulge protectively. "You have three months," she said.

•

At the interview, the museum people were awed. "This is amazing," they said, flipping through the images of severed body parts, burning twisted metal, mass burial sites. "This is," the head interviewer gulped and brushed his hand over a picture of a Sudanese ten-year-old with a machine gun and a Chicago Bulls t-shirt, "this is courageous work."

The combat photographer was used to this reaction. He nodded, made the face he made when people looked at his work—something between humility and gritty determination and recognition that yes, this was courageous work but still, somebody had to do it.

"Are you sure you'll be okay working in a studio?" they said. "Will that be boring for you?"

"If I can thrive in that environment," he said, nodding at the portfolio and making the face he made when people looked at his work, "I think I'll be okay in this one."

The negotiations took all of two minutes. The salary was slightly less than he had made as a freelancer, but of course there was a 401K, paid vacation, flex time, optional life insurance and disability and tuition reimbursement. There was health insurance.

•

The combat photographer marveled at how easy it could be to live as a normal person. Running water, hot meals, eight hours of sleep in a warm, comfortable bed. The combat photographer rode the subway, read the sports section, lingered over morning coffee in the photography studio while the museum filled with school groups, tourists, and families.

In the studio, he had absolute control. No wind, sun, monsoon rain. No bullets biting through the air. He took his time. He photographed the museum's natural wonders, exhibits that were being archived—the skulls of beaked whales, ghost orchids, stegosaurus bones.

His days passed with a reassuring regularity. He ate lunch at noon, took coffee at three, and left promptly at 5:30. He often lingered in the front of the museum on his way out, watching the children gape wide-mouthed at the museum's dinosaur displays.

He thought of the unborn child in his wife's expanding belly.

"You were so right," he said.

She smiled and put her hand over his, then placed it on her stomach. "Two months," she said.

•

The combat photographer was not used to being supervised.

"Could you maybe move a little faster in the studio?" his boss asked one day. "Things are starting to back up a little bit." She waved her hand at the schedule, the line of boxes filled with things waiting to be photographed.

The combat photographer gave her the look he gave people when they were looking at his work.

"Thanks so much," she said. "We're just super happy to have you on board."

•

The combat photographer began to wander. On a warm day he went for a walk and found himself at the Vietnam Veteran's Memorial. He took pictures of things left at the wall, homeless veterans in tattered wheelchairs, older men in sansabelt pants saluting the names of fallen comrades, their hands feeling the marble as if searching for a pulse.

For a few minutes his hands worked on their own, adjusting, focusing, loading another roll of film. And then he looked around. Teachers led school trips. German tourists ate ice cream sandwiches and perused USA Today. Joggers lumbered by. Women pushed strollers.

Six weeks, he thought, until the baby comes.

The combat photographer went back to work.

*

The combat photographer looked at himself in the mirror.
He made the face that he made when people looked at his
work. What he saw was a middle-aged man wincing and
crinkling up his eyes.

*

The combat photographer found himself bypassing the
subway for the four-mile walk home. He took the long way,
through neighborhoods on the outer edge of gentrification.
Occasionally, seemingly out of nowhere, he would find his
heart quickening, the old adrenalin kick in his blood. He
would pick up his pace, walking and then jogging down
streets he had never seen before, like a dog drawn to an
unseen mate in heat.

After a few minutes he would hear the sirens or would
arrive at the accident scene to find two motorists in Dockers
arguing over a fender bender, police filling out forms.

He would put away his camera and trudge homeward.

He tried not to think about what was happening to his
body and mind, to his combat photographer's soul, but
it was a long walk and unlike similar walks he might have
taken in Mogadishu or Kashmir, there was nothing to do
but think.

•

"I don't know if I can do this," the combat photographer

told his wife. "I'm a combat photographer."

"You're going to be a father," she said, and gave him the look she gave him when the conversation was over, the look that said combat photographer, my ass.

•

The combat photographer started drifting into the front of the museum. He took photos of children staring at the stegosaurus, old women in wheelchairs, Japanese businessmen in their suits and shiny hair.

He spent more and more time in the front. Things were happening there, he knew, if you had the patience and the right kind of eye. He found unusual scenes—a young husband and wife arguing in a darkened corner, two school groups staring one another down, security bullying street people out the museum's giant doors.

•

The combat photographer had his three month review. His boss rifled through a pile of pictures he had taken in his first months. "I think you need to spend just a little more time in the studio," she said, tapping the back of his hand with a manicured nail. "Less time in the front."

The combat photographer nodded. He thought about giving her the look he gave people when they looked at his work. But then he looked at the work laid out in front of him—dinosaur bones and flowers and fossils and bugs.

"More time in the studio," he said. "No problem."

•

The combat photographer waited for his cell phone to ring. The baby was two days overdue. He hunkered down in the studio, took what seemed like the same pictures he had been taking for three months.

He fought the urge to go to the front of the museum.

The phone rang. "It's time," she said.

The combat photographer hurried into his office, gathered his things.

The fire alarm rang. He ran into the hall. People were frantic, crying, scurrying toward the back exits. He could hear pandemonium in the museum, sirens getting closer.

"It's real!" a security guard shouted. "Fire in the archives."

The combat photographer walked back into his office. A calm settled over him. He looked at the cell phone, his packed bag. The sirens were just outside. The smoke was getting heavier.

The combat photographer grabbed his cameras and his camera bag. He opened the door and ran toward the fire.

THE FIRES I

The fires came down from the north. Or they drifted in from the west, sparks floating like dandelions over the desert and the mountain streams. Some heard they had started in Mexico, some that they had crossed the Atlantic. At that point, so much had happened, so much had been lost, that the few who remained would have believed anything, and the idea of burning oceans, of fire bubbling out of the ground like water, was almost reasonable. Of course some said it was the government, what was left of it, or aliens or Halliburton or Hollywood, but those culprits had been blamed for everything that had happened already and what good did blame do anyway, at this point? If the fires were coming, they were coming.

●

An ancient man and his adult son huddled in the hay bin of a barn. They had decided earlier that if it started, if the smoke they could see from the northwest was going to burn through what was left of the corn and onto the farm, it would be best, finally, if they went with it.

"Well?" the old man said. He sat on a discarded couch that had been dragged into the barn years ago, when his children had been teenagers.

The son, forty-eight and feeling like an old man in his own right now, stood by the window. "Fire," he said.

The son was a doctor and had spent most of the past

several months roaming the countryside, helping the sick wherever he found them. What he had learned was that everybody was sick, everybody was dying, and there was nothing an obstetrician could do to stem the tide. With nowhere left to go, with his family gone in the first wave of the sickness, he had turned north with no more idea in his head than the opposite direction of the place where he'd buried his family, and hadn't really thought so much about it until he was walking the ghostly halls of his old high school.

An old song had come into his head like an infection that had taken root years ago and lay dormant until this moment: "Magic Power" by the band Triumph. "She's young now she's wild now she wants to be free, got the magic power of the music in me." He stopped at a locker and wondered if it was his old one, if his muscle memory had somehow led him to this place. He put a hand on the door but didn't try to open it.

There was no magic power and the fact that this notion had once held some meaning for him, tenuous but real, was as absurd as the books and notebooks and wrappers that lined the halls. All of it nothing but kindling for whatever was next.

When he got to the farm he was not surprised to find the old man still alive, even though he hadn't seen another live person for over a week. Or a month. Time had gone slippery. Of course the bane of his early existence, the holder of switches and secrets and reproaches was still alive. They greeted one another with a nod. "Did you bring any food, at least?" the old man had said, but it wasn't really a question and the man just grunted and shook his head and looked out the window at the smoke far off in the distance.

They had settled into a routine of watching in the barn and reading their books, cooking one meal a day and pumping water from the well.

Now, for the first time, smoke began to fill the barn. "Is it coming?" the old man said.

The man went to the window. Corn was burning in the northwest. He looked out the other side and was not surprised to see fire encroaching from the south. Why had he come here? The old man had missed a lifetime of accomplishments, of victories and defeats and births and deaths. There was so much to say. "It's here," he said.

SEVEN CLOWNS BEFORE THE EXPLOSION

ARIAL

He is driving, like always, curling the little car in ever-tightening spirals, pushing it, feeling the centrifugal force and allowing the audience to blur in his vision, a whirl of light and color, color and light, a beautiful hallucination, one of many that exist only within the small universe of the circus.

It is the only universe that matters to him and right now he is its god. All eyes are focused on the tiny car that he navigates through the tight, intricate web that is the Astounding Traveling Circus of the World: the elephants off to the right, the center ring to his left, the trapeze artists and jugglers milling off to the side, the zebras and the lion and the tiger and the poor bedraggled dancing bear, the mini-hot air balloon that will carry Lewis the Conductor to the rafters for the grand finale.

He accelerates even as he pulls the car in an increasingly unlikely circle. This is what it is all about, he knows: improbability. It is the joke that this whole circus is built around: a tiger, an elephant, a hot air balloon, right here in Des Moines or Indianapolis or Altoona. Seven clowns and a monkey piling out of a car, one after the other in a tangle of funny shoes and makeup and hobo clothes, and just when you think that there can surely be no more room in that car, here comes another one.

He feels Stumpy's palm on his leg and taps once, a warning. His hands tighten on the wheel. Like the kiss wasn't unprofessional enough. Should never have taken a boyfriend in the circus, he thinks, much less in his own shop.

The audience grows louder, applauding and whooping and whistling, building to the inevitable conclusion. He drives, the calm eye of this particular hurricane. It is what he does. He is a professional.

He would never tell Stumpy, of course, but this, right now, the actual act itself—the audience and the costume and the stupid routine—is the only thing he truly loves.

STUMPY

The car might as well be his own heart, tightening, going faster and faster, bump bump bump, threatening to career out of control at any moment. And he is supposed to concentrate on the audience, the show, with Arial's thighs pushing tight against him?

It is all he can do to fight the erection—not another night like Cleveland, a biological disaster that almost got both of them fired. He doesn't even need the job—Jesus, the job is shit. He could be making better money doing customer service again. But he needs this: the two of them, literally whirling through the world, city to city, thigh to thigh, heart to heart.

He casts a conciliatory glance to his left, but Arial is stone-faced, businesslike as always. And it makes his heart whirl and plunge again to think that he's done anything that could upset this thing that they have, this delicate balance like the reeling car itself—out of control and beautiful.

It was just a peck, a good luck kiss, and he doesn't think anybody else saw a thing. But still, he understands that there are lines that simply cannot be crossed. The circus is a thing of the past and this applies as well to the internal politics, the tightly wound social fabric of the Traveling Astounding Circus of the World. To Arial, a lifer who has never had an email account or owned a computer, a man from a different time, a man who, if there was such a thing, could easily be elected mayor of the Circus, any rupture in this fabric is a Hindenburg occasion.

He breathes in and out. It will be okay. It will be okay because it has to be.

CLIFFORD

Feel your character. Find your center. Breathe in. Breathe out. Be here now. Find your center. Feel your character.

This is not where he thought acting was going to take him, but he reminds himself again that this is a career, a calling, that he is in it for the long haul. He is running a marathon, even if the rest of them are running a sprint, looking for an easy check, drinking and screwing their way across the country in a rambling swath of minor league cities.

Sometimes it is difficult to keep all of this in perspective.

It is the same every night, in every city: the same car, the same clowns, Arial at the wheel, Stumpy mooning to his right, Shoopy and Poppy and Franny and Shorty and Nibbles jammed into the back. The smell of popcorn and elephant shit, the car's exhaust, Stumpy's Axe body spray, Shoopy's sweet alcohol breath and the monkey's musky stink fogging in from the back seat.

Breathe in and out. Breathe in. Breathe out. In. Out.

In.

Out.

Center.

What is your character's motivation? Clifford is a sad clown. Clifford was sexually abused by an uncle who just happened to be a clown. Every night, the young boy would hope against hope that tonight would be the night he would not hear the heavy slap of the clown shoes making their way down the stairs. Every night, the crisp clip-clop of cheap plastic on wood. Every night, the boy would pull up the covers and pretend he was dead, and then, when this failed, he would close his eyes and wait for it to be over.

Everything Clifford does—from his facial expressions to the way he trudges across the stage—stems from this one thing. After every performance, when they are stuffed back into the car and the rest of the clowns are high-fiving or breathing a sigh of relief, unscrewing their flasks or screwing up their courage for the night ahead, Clifford weeps.

There is a price he pays for this—the man behind the clown, the actor. It is a price he gladly pays, like those before him. He is an artist.

SHOOPY

He wishes he could take just one more nip, but it won't do, not again. He burps and takes care to push his Rumplemintz breath downward and to the side, away from Arial, who flat out won't put up with any bullshit. This means he is exhaling directly onto Shorty, of course, but Shorty is way past caring.

Shoopy cares just enough to not get fired. He is forty years old and knows who he is.

There are not many jobs that align well with his lifestyle, literally no other jobs where being at least a little off center, a little buzzed, actually improves your performance. Of course, the problem is keeping to just a *little* off center.

He likes the circus well enough, better than the Xerox job or the sales floor at Best Buy. They travel, work at night. Short hours and a per diem. Plenty of young people who like to hit the bars at night, or play cards in their trailers, easy enough to find a party and not feel so old and used up and stupid about it.

He is comfortable in his own skin. He is not going to be Mick Jagger or Derrick Jeter, isn't even going to be one of those guys in the Memphis Horns, or a journeyman shortstop, a bit player in some bad sitcom. And so this: one of seven men in makeup and funny shoes, jammed into a car.

It isn't exactly a rock star existence, not where he thought he would be, but it's better than nine to five. As long as he can keep it to just a little off center, he'll be fine for now. Still, one more nip would have been nice.

POPPY

He was supposed to be an athlete. A professional. First in districts senior year in high school, gymnastics scholarship to Ohio State, Olympic qualifier. And then the fall on the uneven bars, a shattered forearm, failing grades, the ad on craigslist and here he is, twenty two years old and packed into a car between an alcoholic and a midget, wondering if he'll be able to get the smell of monkey off his forearm before the cast party tonight. Where are they? Pennsylvania or Ohio, rolling mountains and pickup trucks. Altoona, maybe.

He needs to get his resume together. Learn HTML. Maybe art school? He always did enjoy drawing, at least before gymnastics took over all his time. But it's all computers now. Maybe that's good. Maybe not.

Arial is driving a little faster than usual. Pissed off because his little boyfriend kissed him before the show. Like everybody doesn't know they're together. Like anybody gives a shit who is with who, what they're doing in the privacy of their own trailers. They are grown men in makeup who perform the same awful carnie routine every night—every single night for the past, what, like, million years?

Tonight is the night. Get his resume together. That's the first thing.

SHORTY

Of course he's named Shorty. Shorty the Fucking Clown. He had wanted to be Buffalo Bill, had a whole cowboy clown thing happening—a real one, having just come off the rodeo circuit, healed now but the crack in his tailbone still aches if he sits for more than an hour—but then, there they are in the employment office and, like always, like elementary school and high school and the job in the Buttercrust factory, like every time he walks into a fucking bar, he's Shorty.

Life is truly nasty, brutish and, fuck fuck fuck...short. One long string of stature jokes and imbeciles and drunks, one after the other, each dumber and meaner and taller than the last.

Fuck it.

He allows his body to go slack as the car winds in ever smaller circles, accelerating, moving faster, tempting fate to lift it off the ground. He can picture it—the crash, the tangle of limbs, the gasps from the crowd, blood and bones and gristle and fire.

Whatever.

His eyes go unfocused and the audience is nothing but a whirl. The monkey on his lap—of course, the little person has to carry the goddam monkey, right, there's a symmetry in that?—clutches his arm tighter. Too tight. The monkey needs a bath, a nail clipping. His monkeynails dig into Shorty's forearm, leaving eight perfectly matched little cuts and two thumbsize bruises.

Opposable thumbs, he thinks.

Blood oozes. Shorty closes his eyes and feels the little car go faster.

NIBBLES

Bananas! Biscuits. Soon they will feed Nibbles. They will do what they do and then they will feed Nibbles. He is sitting in the moving thing, on the way to do what they do. Sitting on the lap of the small man.

The moving thing goes fast. It turns hard and Nibbles holds onto the small man's arm. The moving thing is going faster than usual. Nibbles is scared. Biscuits! Nibbles is scared.

FRANNY

These homosexuals have not accepted Jesus as their lord and savior. It is a mockery, a sin. This entire circus is going to hell and nobody cares. He ticks the sins off on his fingers: divination and sorcery, fornication, alcohol abuse, blasphemy, atheism, impurity against nature.

Mortal sins, all of them. The circus is a literal Sodom and Gomorrah.

He has been a Christian for one hundred and forty

seven days. At first it was a trial, then a gift, and now, lately, a responsibility.

Of course he suspected, had heard the whispers, seen the winks, the way Stumpy's hand lingered on Arial's thigh. But now he knows. His heart is still beating wildly. Impurity against nature. It is the perfect description. Two men kissing, their stubble rubbing up against one another, cracked lips caked with pancake makeup. It is one of the most disturbing scenes he has ever witnessed, and his reaction is physical, a roil within, a stone he knows he must pass.

"And for their sins they were destroyed by brimstone and fire from the Lord out of Heaven."

Amen.

The car is hurtling toward the big finish. Off to the side, the hot air balloon filling with gas. The car pulls in tighter, coming around for one more circle. He leans forward, past the gymnast and the midget, he pushes his arm past the drunk, over the shoulder of the homosexual. The air balloon is yards away. He turns the wheel.

THE FIRES II

Ronnie sniffed. "Smoke," he said. He pulled the blankets up to his chin and the girl squished down, pushed her head under the covers. "Are you okay?" he said.

She squeezed his hand tighter. "Did my heart love until now?" she said. She stared off into the middle distance, toward the LeBron James poster on the wall. "I swear I never saw true beauty until this night."

He had stopped asking if she thought they should leave, try to make it to the beach or the places he had heard about beneath the subway, back when there were still people to hear things from. He had decided to wait it out, face whatever was coming next and live through it or not, right here in this room. There was a certain poetry to it that he guessed she would have appreciated before whatever had happened to her.

The boy was a few years older, sixteen to her fourteen, or that was what he guessed. He didn't know what she was like before, but there were clues: the way she never used contractions, the filthy Hermes bag she had packed with scarves and underthings that looked like they had been expensive, at one point. Before.

All she would talk about was love—whether they were in it or not, how deeply, the kinds of things she would do if deprived of his love. He guessed she had seen some movie or read some book and when it all started to go wrong, when the sickness came and then the death, the loneliness and the silence and the birds, and now the smoke and sound of something coming—fires or oceans or dragons, he would be surprised by nothing—she had regressed somehow, latched onto something from before and closed up around it like a locket protecting a photograph.

He could feel the heat rising. The smoke had been distant, a hint and then a promise and then all of the sudden it was present, here, as much a part of the room as the LeBron James poster or the peeling paint on the ceiling. He realized in a flash that this was not like the sickness, which had passed him by for reasons he couldn't fathom. "I don't know if we're going to..." he said.

She put a finger on his lip. "Shhhhhh," she said. She sat up and looked again toward LeBron James, frozen in mid-air, his face determined, muscular arms raising the ball over an already defeated defender. "Take him and cut him out in little stars," she said. He knew she was reciting something but couldn't place it. Maybe the movie about the teenage vampires? "And he will make the face of heaven so fine that all the world will be in love with night."

It was becoming difficult to breathe. The words she said were pretty but they were only words. He pulled her close and could feel the sweat on her legs. She burrowed her head into his chest and coughed. He pulled the comforter over their heads and held his breath.

THOSE PEOPLE

We're having our second cup of after-breakfast coffee, Tricia looking through the activities for the day, talking about the benefits of the Down Home on the Blue Dome BBQ versus the parasailing excursion, when we finally see our host. She is short, heavy, skin tanned the color of my two-creamer coffee, hair dyed corn yellow. The first thing we hear is her signature laugh and of course everybody turns toward the Davy Crockett Deck, because we've heard that laugh before on *Cookin' With Sara* or the *Today Show* or *Oprah* or the Walmart ads or, lately, the news shows where we watched the grainy video of her saying those terrible things and then the high-definition Sunday talk apology tour that followed. There's a noticeable rustle and I sit back because, for the first time since we boarded this cruise ship, people aren't staring at me.

She works the room like a politician at a hometown pig roast, looking each traveler in the eye, shaking with two hands, making jokes and small talk and complimenting the women on their clothes or hair, the men on their women. That laugh bounds out toward the ceiling, seeking the open air of the entrances, and I picture each delighted bark slipping out over the ocean like a balloon until it pops and fizzles down into the sea.

"Holy shit there she is," Tricia says. She kicks me under the table. "Sara fucking Lane." She says it like you'd say there it is, Christmas morning," like it's inevitable but remarkable all the same, because of course it is: we are, after all, currently steaming out to sea, three hours out of Miami, guests on the Sara Lane Luxury Cruise.

We are watching. Everybody is watching. "Oh my goodness you have got to tell me your secret," Sara Lane says to an overweight lady who has clearly tried to imitate her signature hairstyle. She twirls the woman's bangs like a hairdresser. "Just darling!" she says, and another laugh whoops up toward the ceiling. She turns to the next table and that's when she sees me. Our eyes meet and her face drops for just a moment, and then she must be realizing where she is, doing the mental calculation of whether I'm some kind of inside man for the NAACP or if I'm just another guy looking to enjoy an all-inclusive cruise with his favorite television chef personality. She smiles and I'm glad I listened to Tricia's suggestion about how to dress today—collared golf shirt, khakis, docksiders. "Just dress like the rest of them are going to be dressed," she had said, and we both laughed even though she was only half-joking.

Sara Lane chugs toward us, her face set in a half-smile, like she's waiting to go to a commercial break. She steps past two tables full of middle-aged couples dressed head to toe in University of Tennessee regalia and they stare in amazement. My face is frozen in a half-smile too and I notice for the first time two black-clad security guys in the back of the room, talking into microphones. They each take a tentative step forward, then another.

"Well my goodness don't y'all just look like a picture!" she says. I stand up and we're shaking hands and I notice how small she is, how orange, how her open-toed shoes pinch at the chubby tops of her feet. "So glad to see y'all!" she says, and I wonder if she really is speaking a little louder, pushing her words out toward the entire Crockett

Deck, or if this is how she talks all the time. It's gotten quiet, the room gone still, and I can hear the steady clink of a bar being set up, jangly country music.

"Y'all mind if I sit down?" Sara Lane says. "Join you for a spell?"

"Of course," Tricia says.

Sara Lane plops down in a chair and the table wobbles, sending a splash of my coffee onto the starched white tablecloth. "I am so sorry," she says. She nods at a waiter— an almost imperceptible gesture, as much will as motion— and he hustles over and replaces my mug.

Sara Lane's face goes serious. "I hope," she says, leaning over the table, locking eyes on me and then Tricia and then back to me, "that you all have been made to feel welcome."

"Um . . ." I say. Tricia nods her head, pushes her hand out dismissively, as if there could never be any question as to how welcome we might feel.

"Not *different* welcome, mind you," Sarah Lane says. "Just...well, you know. *Welcome* welcome."

We nod. In the background, I can hear the busboys speaking in quick Spanish. A laugh from the kitchen. Guy Sterling singing about heartache over the ship's ever-present speakers.

Sara Lane puts her hands on the table, reaches out and covers Tricia's hand with her right, mine with her left. She is small and has to half stand in order to make the distance. Her hand is sweaty and hot and I fight the urge to pull my hand back, stuff it in my pocket. "I want to say something to you," Sara Lane says. Again, she looks Tricia in the eye, and then me. One of the security guys has slipped through the diners and is standing a few steps to my left. "I want to apologize."

Tricia starts to say something and Sara Lane shakes her head no. She squeezes our hands tighter. "I need to," she says. She closes her eyes and when she opens them again they are teary and I wonder if this is some kind of actor's trick. "I want to apologize to you personally. For what I said all those years ago." She closes her eyes again and a tear drifts down her cheek. "I know you saw that video. Everybody saw that video. And I want to apologize for the things I said. The word I used. That was a private party and back in those days I was still drinking and I said something I had no right to say. Whether you all might say that word all the time or not, I had no place." I try to catch Tricia's eye but she is focused on Sara Lane. "But you know what? I'm glad. I am." She looks at us like she is revealing something of incredible importance. "I'm a better person now. I'm not proud of that moment but I'm proud that I'm sitting with you lovely people today. And I'm proud that you're here. That makes me so very, very proud." Her eyes are closed and she opens them and looks at Tricia then at me, then she scans the nearby tables, who have all ceased attending to their eggs and bacon and hot buttered grits and even the signature biscuits. She nods, squeezes our hands again, and sits back in her chair.

Silence hangs in the air. Even the kitchen has gone quiet. Guy Sterling is now singing about horses and I remember that he is here as well, featured performer at tonight's welcome barbeque.

I have no idea what to say and I'm so relieved when Tricia clears her throat. "It's a lovely cruise," she says. "I was just saying to Lionel that it's so hard to choose from all these amazing activities."

"Thank you," Sara Lane whispers. And then she shouts "Thank you so much!" and it's like the sound kickstarts the room—people begin talking again, eating, the room filled with the familiar scrape and tinkle of forks, knives, glasses. Sara Lane stands up. She wipes her eyes. "Y'all really gotta try the biscuits," she says, and waddles off to shake hands with the Tennessee people, picking up right where she left off.

•

Tricia is sleeping and I'm playing a game on my phone when an envelope slips under the door.

We have been upgraded.

The letter is short, a few sentences that describe our new circumstances on Sara Lane Enterprises letterhead, with Sara Lane's swooping signature in real ink taking up the bottom third of the page.

"What is that?" Tricia says. She sits up, sniffs the air.

"A letter," I say.

"What is that smell?" Tricia says. She sniffs again, rolls onto her back and pulls a pillow over her face.

"Dear Mr. Johnson and Ms. Lebout," I read. "I'm happy to let you know that you have been upgraded to a first class suite on the Dolly Parton Deck. Please call the cruise office at your earliest convenience to have your essentials moved to your beautiful new room. Your friend, Sara Lane."

Tricia sits up, reaches out a hand and I give her the letter. "And a shitload of that, what, signature perfume?" she says.

For the first time, I notice the smell. Sweet, almost

syrupy. The letter has been doused in it and the entire little cabin smells like a Victoria's Secret and feels all of the sudden cramped, clammy and fecundant, as if another entity has squeezed itself into our room and began slowly expanding.

Tricia starts pulling her things out of the built-in drawers below the bed, dropping them into the suitcase again. "First class suite," she says. She nods, like it was something that was going to happen all along, like finally it did happen and it all makes sense.

"Are you sure?" I say. "Sure we want to . . ." I can't quite find the words. I look around the little cabin. There's no view and just this one room and the bathroom, and our feet both stick out over the end of the bed, and the one time we've had sex in here we had to cover our mouths to avoid scandalizing the neighbors. But really, it's fine.

"First. Class. Suite." Tricia says.

"I don't know," I say.

Tricia stops putting things in her bag. "Look," she says. "It's not our fault what this lady did. It's not going to make any point if we refuse. Crazy lady got herself into trouble and now she's going to make herself feel better."

"But that's just it," I say. I look to where a window would be but there's just a wall. This room is smaller than my bathroom at home. "Is it just, she's trying to make herself feel better? Or is there, like, something else happening here?"

"Should I have not come on this trip?" she says.

"You're right," I say. I pick up the letter and wave it around like a lottery ticket and the perfume smell wafts up in my face. "Of course you're right."

•

The new room is about ten times larger than the old one, which is to say it's roughly the size of two regular hotel rooms put together. Tricia walks right to the little patio and slides open the doors. Outside, the ocean is loud and gray.

Two porters move our things into the master suite and I stand there with Tricia, looking out at the ocean. We're holding hands and the waves roll one into the next and we can smell the salt air and it really is lovely. I try to tip the head porter and he shakes his head no, pushes the money back into my fingers and stuffs his hands into his pockets. "Orders of Mrs. Lane," he says.

"Are you from the Caribbean?" I guess at his accent.

He pauses, seems to be considering whether to reply at all. "Bajan," he says, finally. "Barbados."

"I thought so!" I say.

"Have an excellent cruise, sir," he says. On the dining room table, there is a fresh bouquet of tropical flowers and a letter on Sara Lane stationary. This one is handwritten and drenched in even more perfume than the first: "I do like to make my friends feel welcome," it reads, "and thank you for doing the same for me. Please be my guest tonight—and guest judge!—at our Guy Sterling Make Your Own Margarita Contest!"

I had been planning to order in room service, have a quiet night in our new room. But the margarita contest is one of the things Tricia had circled on the itinerary. Be spontaneous, I tell myself. Be fun. Margaritas are fun.

Tricia is back to the window and she has her arms folded over her chest. She is beautiful and smart and like a buttress up against the rest of the world and when I'm with her I don't have to worry about anything. "How do you imagine one dresses," I say, "to judge a margarita contest?"

•

A short, middle-aged woman in a business suit comes to tell us that Sara Lane is working late in her office and will not be able to join us. "Well that's a shame," Guy Sterling says. I nod and sip at my water. Tricia slurps from the two-foot-tall concoction placed in front of her like a tropical bird. "But we do have a special treat for you all," the woman says, smiling. "In her place, Mrs. Lane has sent along Olean!"

"Well I'll be," Guy Sterling says. He smiles and drinks from his beer. "I reckon I better get me another one of these here then."

From the entrance, we hear a laugh and then a whoop. The word "Olean" slithers through the room. I turn to Tricia but she is busy talking with Guy Sterling's date, a beautiful thirtyish woman with a Russian accent who has been steadily drinking gin and tonics for the past half hour. I'm trying to put out of my head that my fellow guests almost certainly think I'm some kind of minor celebrity: a hip hop artist, a baseball player, or a bit actor on a third rate cable show. I have been asked to sign autographs, each a shrugging coda to the more exciting prospect of obtaining Guy Sterling's autograph. Tricia has signed them, too, as has the Russian model. They are having a ball, Tricia writing Kerry Washington's name with a flourish, the model writing the letter M with a condescending nod to each supplicant. I feel terrible, guilty. With each piece of paper I sign, I feel like I'm digging myself deeper into whatever this is, one unrecognizable and embarrassed squiggle at a time.

"You're in for a treat now, man," Guy Sterling says. Everything he says sounds like he's reciting a line from a made-for-television western, and this time he actually touches the brim of his cowboy hat and points.

The chatter ramps up and I can track the progress of the new guest by the way people keep popping up from their tables to greet him. It's like tracking a pod of dolphins from the shore: every now and then a little scurry and a table full of people pop up. Finally, he's standing in front of us, a short older man with graying hair and a handlebar mustache. He is wearing a white suit with a bow tie, a modern-day Mark Twain. His eyes are bright, clear and intelligent. "Well I'll be," he says. "If it ain't Guy Goddam Sterling. In the flesh."

Guy Sterling stands. "Olean Goddam Lane," he says. "Still standing."

"I reckon that's enough to celebrate on," Olean says. He twists his handlebar mustache and nods at the waiter. "Bourbon rocks," he says. He introduces himself to Tricia and the model. I realize that we're all standing, that I've stood along with the rest. The old man is familiar, of course: Sara Lane's brother is a frequent guest on her show and a restaurateur in his own right. Lately, I've seen him on the news, defending his sister and explaining how their upbringing might have led her to say the kinds of things she said on that tape.

His bourbon arrives and we sit. He makes small talk with Guy Sterling and I watch Tricia and the model whispering. What could they possibly be talking about? I feel a hand on my own. It is warm, calloused and hard. Hands that have done some work. Olean squeezes and leans over. "Hey man," he says in a low voice. "I just want to say thank you. To you and your lovely girlfriend there."

"Thank you?" I whisper.

"We really appreciate it," he says. "You all helping us out here."

•

We're finished up with the contest, which wasn't so much a contest as it was Olean drinking one margarita after the next, complimenting each passenger on their unique style and slipping out to smoke cigarettes on the deck between drinks. Tricia and the model and Guy Sterling have disappeared, off to check out some other lounge where the model knows the bartender. I've been sipping at margaritas and listening to Olean and Guy Sterling trade stories about everything from the University of Tennessee to fake breasts to the best way to avoid alligators in a Louisiana swamp.

I excuse myself to the bathroom and they both pause, nod, and go back to their conversation. I'm standing in front of a urinal, next to a red-faced, portly man with gray hair and a University of Tennessee shirt. "Quite a time, huh?" he says.

Even in here, the country music trickles, Guy Sterling singing about lassos and love.

"Yes," I say. "Quite a time indeed."

"Old Olean." He says it like an exclamation, like that single word is all one would need to hear, like he's saying "hurricane" or "evacuate" or "guilty."

"Indeed," I say.

I zip up and move over to wash my hands.

"Indeeeeed," he says. He is breathing loudly and I

wonder if I would be able to revive him in the case of a heart attack, a thought I've found myself having twenty times a day on this cruise. "Indeeeeed, says the man," he wheezes, sarcasm dripping into his voice now. He fumbles with his zipper and I realize that he is even drunker than Olean himself. "Mind me asking a question, there, son?"he says.

His voice has changed, the aw shucks washed out with venom, like he's substituted "son" for "boy."

I grab a paper towel and feel for the door. He takes a few halting steps toward me. His zipper is open and his shirt untucked. His face is nearly the same orange as his shirt.

"What the hell did you do to get to sit with the stars, huh?" he says. "Who the fuck do you think you are, anyway," he says, "to be on this cruise, sitting with Guy Sterling and Olean Lane and that lady from the commercial for that car?"

I open the door and he comes closer. In the background, the sound of the ocean and a line dancing country song. "Whothefuckareyou?" he says, and pokes a finger in my chest. My hands are clenched. He is maybe five feet six, two hundred fifty pounds. "Or did you just get a handout? Like how you people do?" he says. I open my mouth to speak but nothing comes out. The ocean roars in my head. "A fucking handout!" he says again, daring me to speak. I'm sweating, my hands shaking. The man smiles but there's no mirth in it. He wipes his hands on his pants, pulls out a pack of cigarettes and slides one between his lips. "Yeah," he says. "That's what I thought."

•

I make my way toward the table, where Guy Sterling and Olean are still engaged in conversation. Their heads are close together, each with a beer bottle and a glass of brown liquor in front of them. I don't know whether I should say anything or not. We have been made to feel welcome, have been told that this feeling is important, and I've had just enough tequila to possibly follow up on these promises.

I get closer and can hear Olean talking to Guy Sterling. "What I don't understand," he says, "is what the hell they're *doing* here." I take a step closer, open my mouth, try to think of something casual. Olean takes a drink, shakes his head. "I mean, thank goodness they are because it'll help, you know. Don't think there ain't been pictures. We ain't fucking stupid, even if she acts like that sometimes." He finishes his drink. "But I mean, seriously, what were they even *thinking*, man, you know?"

"How they are," Guy Sterling says, with a finality that's all the more cutting for how casually he tosses it off. They both nod.

"How they are," Olean says. He gestures to a waitress, a Haitian I've spoken to on more than one occasion. She is pretty and young and this is her first Sara Lane cruise. "Two more, sweetheart," Olean says. She nods and turns toward the bar. Both men watch her retreat. I take one step back and then another. I try to melt into the wall, the way I would in the subway or a holiday party. But it's no use here. I see people staring, wondering why that comedian or baseball player or singer is leaning against the wall while his friends Olean and Guy Sterling drink bourbon.

I sneak to the bar, order three shots of tequila. I drink one and walk out toward the deck with a shot in each hand. Before I feel the salt air on my face, they're gone.

•

It's dark in the room and I stub a toe on a kitchen chair, sit down on the floor. I've left the door open and I don't care and somewhere in the back of my mind, something registers: I am very, very drunk.

"Tricia!" I shout. "Pack your bags we're getting the fuck out of here. These people . . ." The bedroom door is closed, a dim light throwing rectangles on the plush carpeting. I throw a shoe at the door. "I guess I knew it all along but . . . fucking . . ." I search my mind for the right term. All I can think about is that redneck, sticking his finger in my chest. My own silence. The smile on the man's face, his eyes too-close and porcine, like Ned Beatty in *Deliverance*. I throw my other shoe and a light goes on.

I stretch out on my back, look up at the perfect eggshell ceiling. I can hear the white noise of the engines, the ocean in the distance, Tricia moving around, fumbling for her glasses, keys jingling, feet scuffing across the floor. Then something else. A man's voice, whispering. The bedroom door opens and Guy Sterling emerges, holding his hat and jacket in his hand. The model follows behind. He gives me a businesslike nod. "I reckon this here's about the end for you," he says casually, like he is remarking on the color of the all-leather sofa or the consistency of Sara Lane's trademark biscuit. He tips his hat and smiles.

The model sneers. "Some people," she says, and follows Guy Sterling through the door. I know she's right, but for the life of me, I can't put my finger on exactly why.

•

I'm pushing at my signature biscuit, watching Tricia do the same, watching my reflection brood in her dark glasses, when I hear the laugh again. We all hear it and we all stop. She works her way through the crowd in the way we've all grown accustomed to now, pausing and laughing and complimenting and then expertly moving on, a small ice breaker in a dining room full of icebergs.

"What should . . ." I say, but Tricia just pushes her plate away, adjusts her sunglasses, sits sideways in her chair.

"Should we, like, get out of here?" I say.

"Why?" she says.

I stare at her, but all I see is my reflection in her dark glasses.

Finally the orange-y glob of Sara Lane comes into view, her bodyguards close behind. She sits without asking, pours herself a glass of orange juice. "Fresh squeezed," she says. "That's something I insisted on. Some things, I don't know, some people might not even notice."

"Uh huh," Tricia says, in the way she does that's half agreement, half challenge.

"Doesn't mean they're not important," Sara Lane says.

I find myself nodding my head.

"I hear we have a misunderstanding," she says. The honey is gone from her voice, the accent ratcheted down several notches, and she sounds like nothing so much as a judge casually opening a case between two people who should know better. "We'll talk," she says. "Up in the office." She stands and walks toward the back of the dining room.

Tricia shakes her head. "Later," she says. The first words she's said to me since we've been awake. She turns and walks toward Guy Sterling and the model at the bar. Guy Sterling signals the bartender. Tricia leans over and

33

whispers something and they laugh.

I break apart my biscuit, push the pieces toward the edges of the plate. I wonder if there's a way to get off this boat. I wonder if I'll ever see Tricia again after all this. I stand and follow Sara Lane like I have been told

•

Sara Lane sits behind a large desk. Too large. She is sunk down, only a foot or so above the desk, straining to make herself as tall as possible, like a toddler in a passenger seat. "This is not my office," she says, by way of explanation. She finds the level to adjust the chair and shoots up a full two feet, times her stop perfectly so her eyes are a few inches higher than mine. I fight the urge to look under the desk to confirm that her feet are dangling above the floor. She waits, silent while I fidget, and I'm sure it's some kind of negotiating tactic, one of those annoyingly effective practices taught by used car managers and how-to-succeed-in-business books from the Fifties.

I know I should wait her out, that we're in a contest now. But I've never been good at contests, at games. The only one I've ever won, literally, is the one that put me in this chair in the first place.

As the time drew closer, I half expected somebody to put two and two together, to remember that maybe I wasn't the best recipient for this gift valued at four thousand nine hundred and ninety nine dollars. But of course, nobody put two and two together because nobody knew me well enough to do the math. A law office is like an engine, and I was an efficient enough part of that engine to draw no particular interest from anybody—good enough to continue but not exceptional in any way.

I look around the room but can feel Sara Lane staring, still playing her game. "So . . ." I say. "Captain's office?"

Sara Lane smiles but tries to hide it and I know I'm right about the books she's read, the contest I just lost.

"Not today," she says. She leans forward and I know I'm supposed to lean back and I try like hell to not do it, but I'm sure it's there, a faint pulling away, the pissy whiff of submission. "Today this is my office. Today Captain Carver will have to file his logs from some other place. Because today this is mine."

"Right," I say.

"Today. Here. Is where me and you come to an agreement, once and for all."

"I didn't know . . ." I say, looking around at the photos on the walls—ships, men in uniform, a family dressed all in white smiling on a beach somewhere—"I didn't know that we had a disagreement."

She laughs that laugh, bark bark bark, and slaps a hand on the table. "Well I didn't either," she says, her voice full of sunshine and honey, lemonade and sugar cookies. "Until I talked to my brother this morning."

I look at the pictures, the books that line the shelves, the floor under my feet. I search for the words. How to explain. Finally I look up. Her eyes are bright blue, unblinking. Her hair is a yellow haze, teased and sprayed into place as sure as a baseball hat. I realize she is still staring, is fighting the urge to blink. "I don't know what you thought you heard," she says. "But Olean and Guy Sterling have never been anything but respectful toward our friends of the opposite color."

"I heard what I heard," I say. Opposite color?

35

"Did you?" she says. She's smiling again, the sugar returned to her voice. "Are you sure?" She gives me a look like she's offering a way out, like I would be a smart little boy if I went ahead and took it. "Because sometimes, as I'm sure you would agree, you just never can tell."

I have no idea what to say, what kind of contest I'm losing right now. I wait her out.

She has something in her hand but I'm not sure what. She sits on the desk, a full head taller than me now. The thing in her hand is a cell phone, of course—smaller, thinner, more silver than any I have seen before.

"Here's the thing," she says. "Maybe I can give you a little lesson. Show you how things are."

"How are things?" I say, trying for action movie cool, but my voice comes out thin and weepy.

"I text 'stop now' to this number," she says, "and the boat goes dark. No power. Just one text and we're back in the dark ages, drifting on the ocean. Watch out for icebergs!" She screams this last word, slaps the table— icebergs!—and I jump.

"Two words," she says. "I text two little bitty teeny tiny words." She puts the phone down and looks at me.

"You know I'm a lawyer," I say.

"Lawyer," she says, and shakes her head. The tone in her voice is one I've heard before, from relatives and Fox News and good country people, the way of saying "lawyer" that sounds like a curse word or something worse.

I scan the floor. In the corner, a handful of Lego pieces are scattered around and I wonder if they're from the captain's child. Grandchild, maybe. Sara Lane types in her phone and clicks a button. I wonder what Tricia is doing now, if her things will still be in the room when I get back.

Suddenly, a thin, metallic sound, like a lever closing, a quick thunk. Then the lights go out. Then a grinding deep beneath us. The boat shakes, rolls gently, and I'm reminded that this whole time we've been moving, grinding forward, that I've been sitting five stories up in a floating building and never really thought about it until the whole thing stopped. The white noise is noticeably absent, the silence is terrifying.

"Happy?" she says.

The ship drifts left. I can hear the ocean crashing against the bow, so far below us. I shouldn't be here. I should be sitting on some ridiculously named deck, drinking fruity drinks and watching Tricia rub sunblock on her legs.

The ship rolls to the left, to the right. I hear people shouting, alarms sounding deep in the machinery of the boat. "You have to . . . " I say.

"You have . . ."

She holds up the phone. "Make it start up again?" she says.

I nod.

"You have a good . . . what's the way to say it? You have a good sense now how this works?"

I nod.

"This being the world, that is," she says. She stretches herself up as tall as she can be and looks down at me. "There are some people....people of action who make things, make things happen, make jobs, TV shows, biscuits so good your mama's panties would get wet just smelling them. And then there are people like you. Lawyers. Bloggers. Parasites. And that's fine!" She tries to smile but it comes out a grimace. Her hands are clutching her phone so hard they're turning white. "It's fine! It takes all kinds! But when it comes right down to it, lawyer, it's people like me who make the decisions, who make things happen, who get to decide how the story ends."

I stare at her and she stares back and the game has started up again. I blink immediately, look toward the door and the sound of people running in the hallways. Another kind of alarm has sounded. I smell smoke and consider for the first time that this could be more than just Sara Lane showing me who is boss.

"What's that?" she says. "That's not . . ." she stands, then sits back down. She texts and then waits. I smell smoke. People are still running outside, alarms going off. "Shit," Sara Lane says. "Shit shit shit." She taps at the phone and then stares at it, taps again. The smoke is getting stronger and we both stand. She throws the phone at me and it bounces off my chest, takes my breath away briefly and then she is gone and I'm standing in the room alone, listening to people running outside. I picture Tricia sitting in our room on the Dolly Parton deck, waiting for Guy Sterling to come save her, for a porter to carry her bags to a waiting lifeboat. "A good sense of how this works," Sara Lane said. "This being the world."

It's getting harder to the breathe and the boat lists to the left so much that everything falls off the desk, the world tilting under my feet. I pick up Sara Lane's phone and I sit down behind the captain's chair, and I wait.

THE FIRES III

Jake sat in the chair and worked through his back files. There was one that he had always wondered about, a boat insurance client who had kept him on the line and then bailed at the last minute. He wondered if the man was still alive, or the wife, who had been the one to hang up on him. They were almost certainly gone. Everybody was gone.

He picked up the phone and heard nothing, as usual. The dial tone had been such a rich, full sound in his life, the precedent to a call, maybe a sale, a chance to fix a problem for somebody or even to simply connect with another lonely person in the middle of the night. When he had started, the sound had terrified him—so full, insistent, waiting, almost daring him to go ahead and call the numbers and see if he could do it, convince somebody he would never meet in person, whose name had come to be on the sheet in various ways that he never did fully understand, that their life would be better somehow if they entrusted a piece of it to State Farm.

Now he put the phone back in the cradle. He pulled at a loose string on the arm of his red golf shirt. His clothes were starting to fall apart but he had always dressed professionally—khakis and the company shirt—and he wasn't about to stop now. He had been surprised when they stopped showing up for work, first a trickle and then almost everybody and then it was just him and Mr. Hernandez for a week until the man had shaken his hand, calmly walked into the break room, and put a bullet in his head.

That night Jake had walked home and not seen a single person on the street, only a few packs of wild dogs. It was six o'clock in the evening but the sky was almost blacked out by the birds overhead circling in a pattern that seemed ominous and not really real, something out of Hollywood. It was the last time he had left the office. There was a supply of snack food in the break room, and once it became clear that nobody was coming back, he'd found an astounding amount of supplies. The things they kept in their desks—soup and energy bars and packages of chana masala. Tequila and bourbon and gin. He had eighteen tubes of toothpaste left and imagined that unless what was coming was suddenly stopped, the fire changing direction or miraculously put out by a gale wind or a hurricane, he would never leave the building again.

He searched through his notes. He remembered the call to be in summer sometime, when he was on the night shift. Those had been good times. He was an up and comer, working as hard as he could at a job he loved for the promise of a solid future. He was working through the steps, too, making amends, attending meetings during the day and learning his craft at State Farm at night.

It was getting hotter and he took the red shirt off, went down to his undershirt. He glanced quickly at the desks to his left and right but of course nobody was there to scold him, raise an eyebrow or tsk tsk. The roar was getting louder, a sound like a thousand spigots released at once. He wondered if he should go to the roof.

Jake opened a file. "Snyder, Damon H." Pretty typical plan. They had signed up when their son was born. They had good insurance. He wondered if they had thought about it as the sickness set in, if it was a comfort in those final moments.

The smoke was in his eyes, snaking down his throat. He could barely see the motivational poster he had had affixed to the far wall: *Dream Big: your attitude, not your aptitude, will determine your altitude*. He had only wanted to help people. He had never taken a sick day, had worked as hard as he could, taken on every assignment that had ever been offered and given it everything he had.

He placed the "Snyder, Damon H" file on his desk and reached for Mr. Hernandez's gun.

YOU PEOPLE

The funny thing about Captain Kent was that he just didn't seem like the type of guy who would go into the pirate business. He never wore an eyepatch, had two working legs, two equally effective hands, nary a peg or a hook in sight. He carried no sword or gun or weapon of any kind, drove a rusty Ford Escort, and was usually dressed in Dockers and a light blue button down. When it was cold he wore a hat, but it was a Philadelphia Eagles knit cap instead of one of those three point things or a Guns 'n' Roses top hat. The whole time we were temping together at the law firm I never once heard him even mutter the word "aaaargh."

"That's bullshit," he said, when I asked him about it. "That's like asking Jay-Z why he never says 'Word to my homies.' He made quotation marks with his hands. I tried to gauge the Jay-Z reference, if he was poking at me or feeling me out or looking to start a fight, but he didn't even seem to notice.

There was a sea of envelopes in front of us, a stack of label sheets in between. I stuck a label on an envelope and looked at him. "A pirate?" I said. I gave him that look like I was kind of in on the joke and kind of not, like, Give me a little help here.

He just kept sticking labels on envelopes. Slap slap slap. His hands moved quickly, effortlessly. He was a labeling machine. I looked at the bin full of addressed envelopes to his left. It was almost full; mine was nearly empty.

"How are you doing that so fast?" I said.

"At sea," he said, dropping an envelope into the bin with his left hand while his right selected another. "A man gets good with his hands." I detected a very light accent, just bubbling under the surface.

We stood there for a while, the only sound the slap slap slap as the Captain addressed one envelope after another. He whistled something that sounded suspiciously like a sea shanty or a Donovan song.

"Come on," I said. "A pirate?"

He stopped labeling and looked me in the eye. Everything was very quiet. I noticed a light scar running from his left eye socket all the way down his cheek. "If you met me on the high seas, Lionel," he said, "you'd know."

I had a flash of vertigo, felt like I was back on the ship listing side to side, and put my hands on the table to steady myself.

"You okay," he said.

"A pirate. Cool. Whatever," I said. I was in no kind of situation to be making judgments about people. I had my own past to protect.

•

"She is a damsel in distress," Kent said. He swirled his rum around with a finger and licked it. "Lost. At. Sea." He pointed toward the bar, where a group of administrative assistants and clerks from the law firm were gathered around a table of colorful drinks—daiquiris and pina coladas and the kind of whipped cream, foot-tall, umbrella drinks I hadn't seen since the cruise. I finished my beer and did the breathing exercises and focused on the table, the physical object of the glass, the thin layer of yellow liquid shining up at me.

"You alright, bro?" Kent asked.

I am alright, I told myself. "Yeah," I said. "Sorry." I nodded at the women's table. "Which one?"

He looked at me like he was sizing me up and I glanced away, felt my face redden. I pushed at my glasses and waved at the waitress for another drink. "Katia," he said, finally, and then, "don't turn around." He nodded a greeting, moved one finger and pointed toward the women's table like a cowboy.

I didn't have to turn around. I knew who he was talking about. She was beautiful, honey brown hair, green eyes, sharp, intelligent features. She was bossy, with a sneaky air about her, like she had decided the best way to avoid getting busted on whatever scam she was running was to accuse everybody else of running some kind of scam. Twice already she had caught me taking coffee without putting my fifty cents in the till.

For the thousandth time that day, like every day, I wondered what Tricia was doing right now.

"Look, Kent..." I said.

"No," he said.

"What?"

"Captain. Call me Captain."

"Captain?"

"Captain."

I gave him that look again, like, Really?

He just winked. I thought about the things we had been talking about in group: I was on dry land, in charge of my own fate, captain of my own ship.

"Captain," I said. I looked around. Just a bunch of sales-looking guys in ties and short-sleeved shirts, Katia and her group, and me and the Captain. Servers in suspenders and buttons.

"So how do you like the firm?" I said.

The Captain just rolled his eyes. "Is this the kind of, what do you call it, small talk, that you people make? Is that the kind of shit we're gonna talk about?"

We both sat there looking at our drinks. We were together all day.

"So where'd you go to college?" I said.

The Captain humphed. It was an old man humph, world weary, the kind of humph a guy in a wheelchair at the American Legion might give you when you asked if he was in a war. He finished his rum. "I gotta ship out," he said.

•

Katia was sitting on my side of the mailroom table when I got in the next day. She was leaning toward Kent, whispering and smiling. I almost dropped my coffee. She didn't fit in the mailroom at all. She was like an alien in our world of paper and envelopes, boxes and bins and labels. She was incandescent, as unlikely as if a giant squid or a right whale had somehow appeared in our midst. I walked slowly, carrying my coffee in both hands.

"There he is," the Captain said. His voice was enthusiastic, like a salesman who had just seen a mark walk into the showroom.

Katia pointed at my coffee, held out her hand.

"I paid already," I said.

She sighed, moved her hand closer and snapped her fingers. Her eyes were as green as apples.

I fished in my pocket, dropped a dollar in her hand. She turned to the Captain, clapped him on the knee. "Ahoy," she said.

•

After work the next day, he took me to this little place down near the river, a dive bar that was putting on airs at being something more. Two sailors who looked younger than us were sitting at the bar. They were both fat and young and loud, drunk, wearing those silly white suits. The Captain nodded to the taller one and sat down a few stools away. The bartender put a beer and a rum in front of him, and a beer in front of me. We clicked classes. "To Katia," the captain said.

The tall sailor got off his seat and waddled toward the bathroom. "What're you lookin' at?" Kent said.

The sailor smiled and put a hand on Kent's shoulder and before I knew what was happening the kid was on the ground. Kent kicked him in the stomach a few times and then faced his companion. The other sailor stood, backed a step, and started hiccupping. The Captain connected with a quick right and the guy went down. He closed his eyes, playing at being passed out. Kent took a ten out of his pocket, dropped it on the bar, and walked out into the street.

We stood there, him staring at the river, me staring at the door, trying to remember the last time I'd been that close to real violence. "What the fuck was that?" I said.

He lit a cigarette. "Nothing," he said. "I don't know, tradition?"

"Tradition?" I said. "That was battery. Assault. That

was four to six years in a federal facility is what that was." He threw the cigarette into a puddle. "Who the fuck are you," he said, "some kind of fucking lawyer or something?"

·

We finished the address labels and they moved us to a long-term project in another division. The law firm was moving databases and we were tasked with copying stuff from one side of our screens and pasting it into the other. Our boss was a guy who actually had a hook for a hand. He was a fat, middle-aged guy who wore cardigans. Andy.

He sat us down, showed us how to copy stuff from one side of the screen to the other. He gave us a little talk about how important this job was, how pleased the firm had been with our work in the mail room. He seemed to believe everything he was saying, and this made me sad for all of us.

Katia started hanging around our new workspace. She knew everything that was going on with every person in the firm. Of course, the Captain and I didn't know anybody or anything she was talking about. We sat in our room and we talked in incomplete sentences while Katia's remarkable presence graced our unremarkable desks, her sing-songy accent bouncing off the walls of our little enclosure like sunlight in a cave.

The only thing she hated worse than coffee welshers, it turned out, was lawyers.

"Little fucks," she said, "all they do is meet, then bitch about each other, then I need this, I need that and bullshit bullshit."

"Don't even get me started," Kent said. "You do not

want to know."

"Hey," I said, "what's the deal with this Halloween party I hear about?"

"The envelopes," Katia said. "What you were labeling. Every year a big party on the river, Anniversary of the firm."

"And everybody goes?" Kent said. He sounded like he was asking if everybody eats popcorn for breakfast.

She shook her head in a neutral way. "Open bar," she said.

•

We got to be friends, Katia and I, with that strange camaraderie that sparks up around two people who are infatuated with the same third person. We were groupies, a two person Scooby gang devoted to decoding the mysteries of the Captain.

When Kent would go to the bathroom or outside to smoke, we would hash over everything he'd said, playing good cop bad cop on the pirate story, one piece of information at a time.

"Did you know that Somali warlords are attacking UN aid ships?" she said.

"That," I said, "is piracy."

"Isn't it, though?" She crossed her legs and smiled.

"He ever mention Indonesia to you?" I said.

"He talks about some kind of cigarettes he can't get here."

We looked at each other and shrugged.

•

"So what's going on with you and Katia?" Kent said. We were doing the usual, copying little folders from one side of the screen to the other. Every now and then I recognized a phrase, directory or file name—fisheries, SOLAS, Hague rules—that brought a quick shudder.

"Nothing," I said. "We hang out. The three of us. Right?"

"You tell me. You're her little buddy."

Am I her little buddy? I thought. "I'm not her little buddy," I said.

He humphed. We moved folders from one side of the screen to the other. The phrase merit salvage flashed from left to right and I dropped it into a directory called Black Dolphin Project.

"You are totally her little buddy," Kent said. "You're all, like, Gilligan and she's all Mary Ann and Ginger."

"That doesn't even make sense," I said. Although he was kind of right about Katia, how she was like a girl next door and a movie star at the same time, her looks snuck up on you like expensive furniture, what seemed plain on first sight turned out to be meticulously elegant. "Anyway, what do you care?"

He stared, his eyes going watery and faraway. He cracked his knuckles. Finally, he turned around in his chair. "Aren't you a little old to be doing this shit?" he said.

"What?"

"You're, what, like twenty-eight? Thirty?"

"So?"

"So you're too smart to be putting labels on envelopes, copying little folders from one side of a screen to the other. What's your deal?"

This was exactly what I was worried about. I never

should have taken a temp job in a law firm. Especially one that had anything to do with marine law, even the idea of the ocean. I felt like I was falling backwards, like my cheap office chair was sucking me into a vortex, like I was back on that ship listing side to side in the middle of the ocean, frozen in my seat as fire alarms rang. I wanted to crawl under the carpet, to slip into the current of something and let it carry me along until I washed up somewhere else.

"Yeah," he said, nodding his head like I'd just told him the whole ridiculous story. "What I thought."

•

The captain stopped coming to work. No word, no calls, no fake cough and mumbles about being sick. Monday, Tuesday, Wednesday I sat in the room and copied folders from one side of the screen to the other and wondered where he was while I waited for the click clack of Katia's heels on the linoleum.

We splurged and went to lunch at TGI Fridays. "Where the hell is he?" I said. I pushed a fry around in a little glob of ketchup. Katia took a fry, slid it along my chicken sandwich, soaked up excess mayo, and dropped it into her mouth. Like everything she did, it seemed to hardly take any effort at all, and somehow it was very sexy. I flashed on Tricia, swirling a drink with her straw and leaning over to whisper in Guy Sterling's ear. I thought about her things all packed already by the time I got home, the matter of fact way the moving people carried them down to the truck and out of my life for good.

"Lionel," Katia said. She tapped a nail on the back of my hand. "What are we doing?"

"What do you mean what are we doing?"

"All this talking about Kent...I mean, you're my best friend here. And I don't know a thing about you."

"Sure you do. You know I get grossed out by french fries and mayo, that I'm not a pirate."

"Not like that," she said.

I felt my face go hot.

"What happened?" she said.

What was I supposed to say? The truth? That long after they had put out the engine fire and righted the ship, after the emergency was lifted and all other passengers accounted for, they had found me sitting frozen behind the captain's desk, the same way Sara Lane had left me? That I had been treading water ever since, and even as I stuck label after label or copied little folders from one side of my screen to the other, I felt as if I was still rooted in that chair?

"We better get back," I said. "I have a bunch of little folders to move from one side of the screen to the other."

•

The next day Kent showed up as usual. He nodded, dropped his bag, and clicked on his computer. He hadn't shaved and his beard was patchy and soft. "Where's your little buddy?" he said.

"Where've you been?"

"Don't fuck with me today. Either of you. Not. In. The. Mood." The accent, always just a slip of a thing, seemed a little stronger.

"I don't know what's up with you, but it's got nothing to do with us."

"So you guys are an us now?"

51

"Oh."

"Yeah."

I stared at my screen. A directory called International Maritime Bureau stared back at me. For the first time, I thought about opening one of these files, reviewing the cases that I knew were waiting there. I was moving my mouse, about to click, embarrassed to feel butterflies in my stomach, an electric tingle on the edge of my fingertips. I caught a flash out of my right eye, felt his palm pushing my head forward and then I was moving, smashing into the computer screen—*pop, crack*. Pain on my forehead. Tears in my eyes. My nose was bleeding and my heart was pounding. I heard the scrape of a chair, his footsteps clipping toward the elevators. I pulled back, put my hand up to my forehead and it came away bloody.

The monitor had a little nose-shaped smash almost directly in the center. To its right, I could still make out International Maritime Bureau. The urge to click on the directory had passed. I wasn't a lawyer, not anymore. I wasn't much of anything

●

We met in the breakroom. She was standing by the side, pretending to listen to two other assistants talking about what they'd wear to the Halloween party. "Go now," she said to the other women. They immediately stopped talking and shuttled out of the room. I poured a cup of coffee, instinctively dropped two quarters into her hand. She shook her head, placed the quarters back into my palm. Her hands were warm. She touched my band-aid.

"Fucking Kent—" I started.

She leaned in and kissed me. I felt like I was floating on the inside of an air balloon, warm drifts carrying me higher and higher. Her lips were the softest things I'd ever felt. Her breasts pushed against my chest. She put a hand on my side.

When we pulled back, she was smiling. "What happened to your head?" she said.

"Kent—" I said.

"No," she said. "No Kent. Not now."

"It's just…"

She kissed me again and for the first time in months I reminded myself to just be.

•

The photocopier went missing. One day it was there, the modern day watering hole of Shipman Admiralty, the next it was gone. Andy clomped up, tapped his pincer on the desk between us. "Anybody know anything about this?" he said. "Kent?"

The Captain smiled, kept on moving folders from one side of his screen to the other.

Andy lingered a few seconds. He stared at the space where the copier had been, looked back at Kent. Finally he stomped back into his office and closed the door.

•

As we got closer to the Halloween party, things kept disappearing. Strange things. A water cooler. A urinal. All of the paper from the third floor. At the same time, people started spending almost all their time talking about what they were going to be for the party. Even Kent and I could tell that the office was on a slow boil, like a high school leading up to a big game.

"They are going crazy," Katia said. "They have no idea how this thing is happening. They are talking security cameras, extra guards, maybe real police."

"During the party?"

"Like they will wake up on Sunday and the building will be gone."

Kent grinned. "You guys have plans for the party?" he said.

•

We met at the bar down by the river. Katia and I decided to put our cards on the table: we were dressed as pirates. When we walked in, he was sitting at the bar in his usual work clothes—the tan pants and light blue shirt. His eyes were veiny and red. There were six empty shot glasses and a little pile of money on the bar.

"It's black Johnny Depp and Keira Whatshername," he said. "Very nice."

I forced a laugh. Katia backed up behind me. We were both nervous for very different reasons.

"What are you?" I said.

"What kind of question is that?" he said. The bartender dropped three beers on the bar, put a shot in front of Kent. "Can't you tell?"

"Um…." I said. I gave a beer to Katia, drank half of mine in one pull.

"Well I'm a fucking pirate, too," he said. "Aren't I?"

•

Kent led us to the party boat, a cruiser that the company had rented for the night. They had decorated the whole thing and it looked like an evil floating birthday cake.

I hesitated at the entrance and Katia pulled at my hand. "Come on," she said. "What's wrong?"

Was it even possible to tell her everything that was wrong? I squeezed her hand and put my head down, watched the backs of Katia's feet as we moved from the safety of the riverside to the deck. I wiped sweat and told myself to just be. Just be just be just be.

Men and women in costume milled around on the deck, smoked cigarettes, drinks in hand. Kent walked to the bar and ordered three beers and three shots.

"Here's to us," he said. He drank his beer in one gulp, followed it with the shot. "Come on!" he said, waving at our full beers, the shots still resting on the bar. "What's wrong with you people?" He was trying to sound funny, but there was no mirth in his voice. The accent was stronger.

Katia put a hand on his shoulder. "What's going on, Kent?" she said.

He stared at me. "I have to go to the bathroom," he said.

We waited at the bar, saying nothing. I felt stupid and cheap in my pirate costume. People kept coming up to Katia, trying to talk, but she just gave them a look, some kind of message conveying like a dog whistle, and they disappeared into the crowd. Kent was gone a long time. "Something's not right," she said, grabbing my hand. "You should go find him."

As I turned, I saw a flash, heard a series of pops.

Suddenly, the dancefloor was a tsunami of people rushing toward the exits. For a moment I was frozen and I heard those words again—"this is how the world works." Then Katia pulled at my hand and I was swept up, moving along with the crowd. It smelled like the Fourth of July, sounded like being inside a waterfall. The woman in front of me was dressed like a Playboy bunny. To my right, a policeman, construction worker, and Indian in full Village People regalia ran as fast as they could in their platform boots. People were crying and praying, pushing one another, falling down. Smoke was everywhere. I stepped on the human resource manager's hand as she tripped and got swallowed up by the rush.

We thronged down the galleyway and onto the street, the river lapping gently at the banks. We gathered in small groups. "Stay with your sections!" a woman dressed as a devil shouted.

"This isn't a fire drill," a guy in a ghost costume yelled. "It's a fucking terrorist attack!"

I walked to a stand of sickly trees and puked. At least I had moved this time. I had run, allowed myself to be pulled into the current. I had wound up here on land, on my own two feet, safe and sound. Captain of my own ship? Katia was walking toward me.

A horn blew and we looked toward the boat. Kent was on the stern, wearing a cheap pirate costume, identical to mine, with its felt eyepatch and three-point hat. He brandished a fake sword. I noticed another sound, the churn of engines, and the boat slowly moved away from the riverside.

Kent took a drag from his cigarette and threw it behind him and flames immediately leapt up, smoke billowed from the center of the boat.

We watched him move slowly away from the harbor, listened as people called the police or the fire department, whispered into their phones.

"There's something I have to tell you," I said. "A lot of stuff."

Katia put a finger up to my mouth. "It's okay," she said.

The Captain grew smaller and smaller. We heard sirens in the distance. The smoke was getting thicker, flames curling toward the sky. Finally, the boat ran aground on the other side of the river, and we couldn't see him at all.

THE FIRES IV

Arial checked their provisions. There was not much left. If this really was it, if the sound in the distance was fire as he suspected, maybe it was a blessing. The monkey was standing by the window, shrieking and jumping up and down, some instinct kicking in now that it was almost surely too late. The only word for it, really, was "shriek." Arial would not miss that sound.

He separated their food into two piles. Their last meal would consist of hot dogs, Mike and Ike's, and barbeque potato chips. "Nibbles!" he shouted. "Nibbles eat!"

The monkey steadied himself and turned. He wobbled toward Arial and sat down in front of the food. The monkey liked Mike and Ike's, and Arial had been saving them, should this moment finally arrive.

The smoke was getting thicker. The sound increasing. They had made it through the accident and the sickness and the time after, had roamed the countryside and managed not to be killed by the gangs or the loners or the dogs.

It may have been more humane to shoot the monkey, put him out of this misery, but Arial knew he could never have done it. He was an entertainer. A clown. At least he had been able to find his life's work and devote himself to it, hadn't been one of those people living one life and secretly or not so secretly wishing they would have chosen some other path. The circus had given him everything: a home and a career and a calling. Even love, if only for a few months.

The monkey had finished his food and had settled down. Did he know what was coming? Could he? Arial picked up his Mike and Ikes and put them in the monkey's palm. Opposable thumbs, he thought. And look where it got us.

The monkey swallowed the candy whole and ran to the front of the store. Arial couldn't see through the smoke. The monkey ran toward the back, then the east wall, then the west. He jumped up and down and shrieked again as the windows began exploding. Arial watched as the monkey sprinted out the front door, the sound of his shrieking receding immediately as the fire's roar entered. Ariel turned a Mike and Ike over in his mouth. Cherry. Stumpy's favorite flavor.

LAWN MAN

They called him Lawn Man. "Lawn Man don't give a fuck!" they would shout, as he pushed the mower up and down the grassy expanse around the big house. He knew they were referencing something, some movie or show or internet thing he didn't know about, but Fernsler didn't care. He would give them the finger, hold it toward the source of the noise while he kept his eyes on the always straight rows of fresh cut grass, and they would cheer and send one of the younger ones out to give him a beer, which he drank while making his way down the next row. He would throw the cup toward the big porch where they liked to sit in their chairs and watch him mow, or toss the football back and forth, or talk to girls or play on their phones, and it would start again in a few minutes. It was an okay enough way to pass the time, and he needed to be out there anyway, cutting their grass for the nine fifty an hour Reichenbach paid and proving to Mr. Thayer that he could hold down a job without breaking the terms.

He could see movement in the big front room where he would wait later while they texted and shouted and called people to track down the one who would pay him. A few of the windows slid open on the upper floors. He recognized most of them by now, the ones who shouted Lawn Man, at least: the one with the red hair, the fat one, the twins, the one with the New York accent. He knew they were students but only a few looked old enough to be in a bar. None looked like anybody at Stoney's or the Creek.

He made a pass along the edge of the yard and the red-haired guy leaned out a first floor window, shouted "Lawn Man don't give a fuck!" There was a round of cheers and Fernsler held his middle finger up and soon enough, there was a kid waiting with a red cup full of lukewarm beer.

By the time he got to the back they had lost interest and he relaxed. There was no audience but their parents' cars and the recycling stacked high with Yuengling cans. He thought about meeting Reichenbach and the rest of the guys at the Tavern. He usually kept to himself, but something about this job, the fraternity house, always made him want to be with people for a little while at least.

He was finishing up the final row, thinking about his meeting with Mr. Thayer and the things he'd have to say: no I haven't been drinking, yes I been working, no thoughts about fire or problems with the gasoline, no angry thoughts or even thinking about anything much at all, really, yessir, gods honest. He pictured Mr. Thayer nodding his bald head and scratching away at the sheet on his clipboard, each of them just filling up boxes, passing the time until they could go about their own business, until Fernsler either got himself in trouble again or he didn't.

He was rounding the corner, just about finished with the back, when he saw her: blond, tall, wearing cutoff shorts and a Penn State t-shirt. She was holding a red cup and waving. He left the engine running, walked to where she was standing.

She smiled, handed him the cup. "From Rusty," she said, pointing toward the house. "Red haired guy?" she said.

"Oh," Fernsler said. He felt like he should say something else but couldn't imagine what that would be.

She pushed the beer closer and he took it and watched her walk back toward the house. At the door, she waved. He held out the beer like he was toasting, then finished it as the door closed.

•

Fernsler went home and turned on the television. He put his Budweiser next to the chips. He had all this time stretching out in front of him at night, a five AM alarm in the morning. It was more like the eighteen months in Rockview than it wasn't, and for no reason other than to fill the time, he had started watching television. He'd never really paid much attention to it before. It seemed like something other people did, sober people with dining rooms and parents who went to bed before Letterman and woke up before school was supposed to start.

Most of the shows were stupid and what he understood of the news was awful. But then he found *Friends*. It was pleasant enough to look at—the two blondes and the sharp, good-looking brunette—and it seemed like there were so many episodes he would never be in danger of seeing them all. He had missed it the first time around—even if there had been a television in any of the houses he grew up in, he doubted they would have been tuned to *Friends*. Now he watched it the way other people watched the news: he hated it, hated everything about it—it drove him crazy and he watched every chance he got.

He clicked over to the station that ran *Friends* from seven through nine, hoping for one he hadn't seen yet. This one seemed to be something about a cat. The funny blonde was singing and Ross and Rachel were mooning at each other as usual. He went into the kitchen and brought back three more beers. Fucking Ross and Monica and their rich parents, their expensive sweaters that they never wore more than once. Fucking Chandler with his hot mom and silly office job. Fucking Rachel and the other one who wasn't as good looking as the others, supposedly working waitress jobs and living on, what? On tips from coffee? Fernsler finished a beer and watched Chandler and Joey leaning back on the same recliner. Joey was supposed to be the poor one, and even he had a bullshit job. Actor. He wasn't mowing lawns, doing dishes, ripping up the visa bill without opening the envelope, writing checks to the apartment management company the day before payday and hoping. Fuck them. He finished a beer and turned up the television. Fuck all of them.

•

Fernsler knew they were gone for the summer, but didn't expect it to be so deserted. First he picked up the trash—red cups and beer cans, mostly, mixed in with sandwich wrappers and chip bags and a few textbooks. Graduation party, Reichenbach had explained. There was a pair of women's underwear and Fernsler thought about putting it in his pocket but remembered how they would usually sit in those windows, watching him, shouting "Lawn Man don't give a fuck," and he put them into the container with the rest of the garbage.

He wasn't being paid to pick up trash, but after the first time, the time they weren't sure and had charged him with public mischief, he had done his public service working for the town, and that was real trash, stink and broken glass and people's perfectly good things and all the feelings that made him feel—so he didn't mind so much picking up Solo cups and panties off a lawn. Here he was at least getting paid, not standing by the side of the road with a vest on that might as well have said "asshole." It would be better, though, still, if there was a kid standing off to the side with a red cup full of beer.

They had paid Reichenbach in advance for the summer, as simple as one kid's signature on a piece of paper, so at least he didn't have to go inside and stare at his shoes while they came and went and texted each other to find the one who would pay. He fired up the mower and made a single pass along the outside, a giant square, then cut a line over to the corner. A light came on and then went out along the hallway on the first floor. Reichenbach had told him the place should be empty but sometimes they came back for a party every now and then, or the town kids snuck in and did whatever they did. Fernsler's job was the lawn, and Reichenbach made it clear his attention should stay on the ground.

When he passed the big room on the first floor, he caught a glimpse of what was inside, two people on the bed, on top of each other. The next time, he knew what to expect and saw a little more, a few seconds of the view. The girl's top was off and she was on top of the guy, who judging from the red hair he was pretty sure was the one they called Rusty. On the third and fourth passes, what he saw was the back of the girl's head, moving up and down. On the fifth pass, Rusty gave him the thumbs up.

•

Fernsler turned up the volume. He had never lived in New York, never even farther away than Altoona, but he was pretty sure dipshits like this would not be able to afford these kinds of apartments in any kind of real city.

Now they were having another one of their fancy dinners. Monica was supposed to be some kind of cook and they did this way too often, all of them together in their outfits and clean skin and perfect hair, none of them worried or hungover or not sure about where to sit or what to say.

He could hear his neighbors, college kids from one of the Asian countries, laughing and shouting through the walls. There were three of them and he could never figure out who was with who: sometimes the one with the glasses seemed like he was the boyfriend, sometimes the one with the long hair. If he could understand what they were saying, maybe it wouldn't be so goddam annoying. Maybe it would be more like watching *Friends* and he could follow along, listen in as Asian Ross fumbled to court Asian Rachel.

Onscreen, the real Ross was giving a toast, thanking his sister, Monica, and his girlfriend, Rachel. Now they were smiling at each other like idiots, or like they had finally figured out how nice it was what they had, how they were all rich, good looking Friends.

Fernsler finished his beer and let it drop on the floor. He thought about eating dinner, but there wasn't anything easy in the fridge and no money for pizza. It was nine o' clock.

•

The girl called it a sex on the beach, and when she handed

it to Fernsler she smiled like she knew it was stupid but liked it anyway. Jenny was her name and she was tall and blonde and would have fit in pretty good in that stupid coffee place, Central Perk, where the Friends traded jokes and moved their plots along. He stole glances at her and tried not to think about her head bobbing up and down through the curtains.

He was less sure about the guy, Rusty, the big one who started the Lawn Man thing and called him 'guy' and 'friend' and said everything like a game show host, like there was some audience somewhere out of sight.

"Wait wait wait!" Rusty said now, pointing to Fernsler's drink. He reached into a plastic bag and came away with a paper umbrella, fixed it to the top of the red cup. "Now it's a proper summer drink," he said, and made a gesture that Fernsler translated as "drink."

He sipped and then gulped. Peaches and vodka and something else sweet. "Pretty good," Fernsler said. He drank again. Already he could feel the alcohol in the back of his head, something starting up slow, but starting. It was pretty fucking good. "Pretty fucking good," he said.

"Right?" Jenny, said. She slapped the table and gave the finger to Rusty.

"Hey, watch out," Rusty said. "That's Lawn Man's move."

"Fernsler," Fernsler said.

"That's Fernsler's move you're rocking right there," Rusty said.

They were sitting at the big table in the side room, the one with all the big pictures. Fernsler couldn't stop looking at all those pictures—each single frame filled with twenty or thirty of them, all wearing the striped blue and red tie, with a year—1975, 1987, 20004, and on and on—in big type right in the middle. He liked the way the hair styles changed as you moved across the years, and then they came back. He liked the way most of them had one guy who was the wacky guy, wearing a funny hat or making a face. He pictured those wacky guys now, pointing out the places where their lawns weren't mowed right, sending back their food, hurrying from one place to the other in their ties and brown pants and tucked in shirts and not a wacky hat to be seen.

"This is an auspicious start," Rusty said. As usual, he pushed his voice out toward some studio audience, waited for the laugh track. "I told Jen we'd find some cool summer friends and sure enough, here we are with the Lawn Man."

"Fernsler," Jenny said.

"I really gotta get to finishing that lawn," Fernsler said. "Before it gets dark out."

"Here's to summer friends," Rusty said. He extended his cup and they toasted. Fernsler finished his sex on the beach. He looked at the grass, black-green in the dusk. He held his cup out and Jenny poured.

●

Fernsler put his six-pack on the table and turned on the television. Monica's mother thought she was a fuck up, called fucking up "pulling a Monica." The last time he had gone out with Reichenbach and the rest of them, he had overheard Bates and Old Snyder whispering about something getting all Fernslered up, and every time Monica's mother said something awful, he took a gulp and wiped his brow and was surprised to find that he was sweating.

The Friends all looked so clean. Fernsler could smell himself, grass and sweat and gas and beer. He went into the bathroom and washed his hands again. He took a shower and went back to the TV. When he finished his last beer, the smell was still on him.

•

Fernsler worked through his first three jobs and got to the fraternity early. He started the mower, acted like he was waiting for it to warm up. He checked the gas, went through the motions of what he'd do to check the oil. Nobody appeared on the big patio, nobody opened any windows.

He stood there for a moment and then realized he didn't have another plan, that he was standing behind a running lawn mower and staring at five inches of rolling fraternity lawn. And there was Reichenbach to think about, the meeting with Mr. Thayer on Wednesday. He cut a line from the sidewalk over to the edge of the house, then followed the edge over to the doorway. He paused when he got to the big room on the first floor. As usual, the curtains were open a few inches and he could see inside, where the girl was sleeping.

She was on her belly, on top of the sheets, her blond hair spread out like a sunset around her perfect face. She was wearing a tiny little shirt and no pants, her underwear riding up on her backside. Fernsler thought about knocking on the window, about sneaking into the room and closing the curtains, sneaking out without waking her. He wondered what it would be like to be out at the Tavern, drinking sex on the beaches and watching her slap the table, give the finger to him in that funny way while Reichenbach and Snyder and even Mr. Thayer watched.

•

Fernsler wondered which of the Friends he could beat in a fight. Chandler and Ross, definitely. Joey he wasn't sure. Was Joey supposed to be some kind of boxer? Or was that the guy who looked like him on *Taxi*?

On the screen, Ross and Rachel kissed. Fernsler imagined himself busting down the door. He would separate them first, say "whoa buddy, whose woman you think you're looking at there?" Ross would make a joke or his stupid puppy face. Fernsler would make sure Rachel was okay, walk her to the sofa, sit her down. He would turn his back to Ross, even, knowing he wouldn't do a thing.

He would give Ross a chance to take the first swing. As soon as he started to wind up his fist, Fernsler would head butt him. When Ross recoiled Fernsler would say something like "who's laughing now, funny boy?" and he would punch Ross right in the face with one hand, and then the other, and he would keep on doing it until Rachel begged him to stop.

As he dumped the gasoline around the room, she would look at him, at first questioning and then proud. They would make out, her chest full and warm against his, the fumes pushing up into their heads. He would light the match and take her hand.

•

"You been staying out of trouble?" Mr. Thayer said.

Fernsler nodded.

"Still doing the landscaping. Working for mister…
Reichenbach?"

"I am."

"Anything new? You keeping a low profile? Got it
under control?" Mr. Thayer took off his reading glasses
and looked Fernsler in the eye. This was his big question.
Fernsler knew he was just looking forward to getting out
of there, that he'd be bellied up at Sharkie's in a half hour.

Fernsler nodded.

"You keep up the good work," Mr. Thayer said.

•

They had been drinking on the patio for a few hours,
Fernsler and the girl with their sex on the beaches, Rusty
and a new guy trading swallows off a bottle of scotch. The
new guy was older, maybe forty, with a beard and long pants
and glasses and a grumpy air about him that made Fernsler
think he was some kind of professor. They introduced
him as Hunter and Fernsler wasn't sure whether that was a
first name or last but he was guessing at first.

Hunter and Rusty were talking about some book and
Fernsler had Jenny to himself. It was easy to talk to her,
especially after two or three sex on the beaches. She asked
questions and he answered them. She told him stories about
people he didn't know and he laughed. Every now and
then she stood up and stretched and Fernsler's entire body
felt like it needed to shiver and he wanted to hit something.
Then she would sit down and ask him a question or tell
him about some party she had some time with people he

couldn't picture and would never meet.

Fernsler felt exposed there on the patio, with the lawn half-done and the mower sitting in the middle and Reichenbach's tendency to drive around in his truck in the afternoons, checking up. He would have to either finish up in the dark or come back first thing in the morning. He could break the machine, bring it to Reichenbach in the morning for fixing, but that seemed like a worse excuse than Jenny, sitting there in her short shorts and her tan stomach and the thought of her ponytail moving up and down in that big room on the first floor.

Fernsler finished his sex on the beach and poured another from the pitcher, then topped off Jenny. "Yes," she said, and slapped her hand on the table. She made a face like she was making a joke and laughed. Fernsler didn't get what she was getting at sometimes, but he was sitting here drinking sex on the beaches and watching her stretch and listening to her stories and he didn't care.

Hunter and Rusty stood. "Hey we're gonna..." Rusty said. He looked at Jenny like she could hear the rest of the sentence in her head.

"Yeah yeah," she said. "Me and Fernsler are good to go."

Me and Fernsler. He sat up then sat down again. The lawnmower needed to be put back into the truck. He would have to do that later, then drive over to Reichenbach's and try to sneak it into the garage. She was telling him about horses now, riding lessons. She sat back in the chair, her bare feet up on the table, her legs long and tan and muscular. Her shirt was too small and kept on riding up, revealing her flat, bare belly. "You believe that?" she said, and put a warm hand on Fernsler's shoulder.

71

Fernsler felt it again, the need to shake himself like a dog. He stood and walked to the edge of the patio and looked out over the trees to campus. The sun had just gone down and the buildings glowed pink in the distance.

"What you doing, Fernsler?" Jenny said.

She was standing next to him before he realized she had gotten up. There was a fair amount of liquor in those sex on the beaches, he thought. She put a hand on his back and he flashed to Phoebe and Monica and Rachel. Before he could allow himself to wimp out, he turned to Jenny and kissed her.

"Whoa what the fuck?!" It was Rusty, standing by the door with a bong in his hand. Fernsler backed up. Jenny had a hand on her mouth and she looked more sad than anything.

"Fernsler, I…" she started.

He ran past the professor, smirking like Chandler or Ross, past Rusty standing there with his hands on his hips shouting something out toward whatever studio audience he wished was watching, past the lawnmower and the truck and the trees lined just right along the summer streets.

•

Fernsler stared at the television. He tried to let his mind go blank, a trick he'd learned from his first cellmate, an Asian guy who was in for dealing. He had called it meditation but to Fernsler it was just spacing out, making the time go as quickly as possible. He had finished all the beer and knew he wouldn't go out for more, couldn't face the streets and the students who would be making their way from one place to another. He stared at the screen, tried to let his mind go, but even with the beer there was something in there that wouldn't unlatch.

He closed his eyes and leaned back. On the television, Chandler cracked a joke, Joey said "how *you* doing?" The studio audience laughed. Fernsler felt like he was rising, moving upwards. He opened his eyes and he was floating over the apartment, *that* apartment, could see the tops of their heads, Chandler and Ross watching television while Monica worried over a pot of something. He couldn't see them but knew that Rachel and Phoebe would make their entrance soon, that a pie would drop and Chandler would make a joke and what seemed like a big dilemma would just bring them all closer together. He saw another figure sitting at the table, wearing a familiar baseball hat. He could smell gasoline and thought about shouting, telling them they better be careful. He could feel the heft of Rachel in his arms, could smell her hair and feel her taught body against his as they made their way down the stairs, the sound of sirens getting closer, smoke filling their lungs.

•

Fernsler leaned back and clicked on the remote. In the distance, the first sirens tearing down the street. The television was large and flat and the sound was wired into the speakers. This is how they lived, he thought. Even in this in-between place they had flatscreen televisions and pretty blond girlfriends and friends who came over for sex on the beaches and in the end they all knew everything would be fine—*I'll be there for you*—no matter how many pies dropped on the floor, whether the lawn was mowed or Mr. Thayer checked this box instead of that one.

He clicked around until he found an episode of *Friends*. The Friends were larger on this screen, more clear, almost lifelike. Fernsler took off his shirt. The gas smell wafted up into his nose and he held it like a bong hit and finally exhaled when he couldn't hold his breath any more. He found one of Rusty's shirts on the floor, smelled it, and put it on. The sirens were getting louder.

He turned up the volume and it was almost like he was really there this time. It was almost like any minute she would come home and find him and he'd make some lame remark and she would crack a joke and the studio audience would laugh and laugh and laugh until the screen went dark.

THE FIRES V

The writer sat under the Rothko where she had spent most of the past few days. She picked up her notebook, opened to where she had left off. She tried to read the most recent paragraph but could only make out the last sentence, which she'd written in all capitals and underlined: AND NOW FIRE.

Her eyes watered and she felt the smoke creeping into her throat, soft and insistent like a drizzle turning to rain. She wondered how long she had. Hours? Minutes?

She first made her way to the museum to save the Rothkos and the Picassos and the Lichtensteins. She had remembered one of the wars, one of the old ones, the television wars, news stories about ancient artifacts being looted from a museum in Egypt or Syria. She wondered if the same had happened here in New York, but of course with almost everybody dead, there was nobody left to make that kind of trouble. She wondered if what happened was a war, an ingeniously evil biological strike by the North Koreans or Russians or aliens. The television had wondered the same thing when there was still television.

She walked to the opposite wall, where she could see the Rothko, and sat down. It was beautiful, the large scale and intimate humanity, childlike colors and bleak exposition. She had tried to do some of the same things with her own work and thought she had achieved a version of it, at least, with the second novel. She was in the same neighborhood, maybe, making her way toward that place.

She had only been in New York for two days, had read at a bar in Brooklyn and was supposed to meet with her editor about the third book when the news started reporting a pandemic, warning that everybody was to stay inside. It had happened so fast—mass exodus, traffic jams and chained hospital doors, and then bodies in the streets and a flicker on the television, static on the radio, the birds and the rot and the smells and then finally she heard the fires coming.

For a while she had entertained an idea that others would make their way to the museum, wait out their last days as some kind of salon, artists and thinkers gathered around some of the greatest pieces of art ever made, celebrating the importance, the permanence of art even in the face of whatever continued to befall them. "Rome is indeed burning," she would say, "and for now, fellow artists, let us fiddle."

That was when she still thought there were others, when she was still working on the third novel, working faster than ever, writing some of the best sentences she had ever written. Now she flipped through the notebook. Words words words. She ripped a page, let it drop to the ground. She was sweating. The room seemed to be dripping, little flames alighting like pigeons here and there. She rolled the notebook up like a cone and thought of the Statue of Liberty. She coughed once, then again. She checked her feet to see if they were on fire. Everything was so hot. She regarded the painting through watering eyes. She did not have much longer. She touched the end of the notebook to a flame and walked to the Rothko. She placed the flame in the corner and watched the colors begin to melt.

FLIES

The first time was at the coffee maker. He was hungover, thankful he'd managed to prepare the coffee the night before—a vague memory, water and scooping and wiping the counter—when he noticed a few small flies drifting around the area. Tiny little flies. Fruit flies.

Typical, he thought, Karen had left something out that had attracted fruit flies. Two weeks. The timing seemed right, long enough for a pineapple slice or a disregarded salad or an overflowing garbage can to have that kind of effect. He was probably better off now.

He punched the brew button, swiped at a fly moving lazily over his head. The coffee was brewing. It was 8:25 and he was supposed to be at work by 9:00, but he knew Paul was out at a client. Everything was fine. He returned to bed.

•

When he got home from work, they seemed to have multiplied. They were there by the coffee maker, same as before, but also flitting around the kitchen window. A lot of them. A squall of them. He swatted, clapped his hands, looked at his palms and saw that he'd come up empty. How was that possible? They were flying all around the kitchen in waves, little loose clouds of them forming along the window and the cabinets, the refrigerator and the entryway and the metal "Love" sign Karen had hung along the back

77

of the kitchen.

All along the windowsill, little black spots. On the walls. The cabinets.

He poured a bourbon and sat down. Jesus, he thought, what did she do? He looked at the refrigerator, the cabinets. Could she have left something in there that would have drawn these flies? Would she have?

He took a sip of bourbon. And then another. He watched the flies circle around the sink area. There was a beauty about it, all those little bodies ranging in and around one another, drifting in constant motion, every now and then alighting on the windowsill or refrigerator or cabinets.

He reached into the freezer for ice and they scattered, swam up, around, over his head. He swatted and clapped and looked at his hands. Nothing.

Fuck it, he thought. If she was here it would be one thing, but gone two weeks and not so much as a text message was a very different thing.

It was typical. She had never been very good at her side of the relationship, the part where the refrigerator is organized, where the cabinets are always full, where there's never a rotten banana or a pineapple slice hiding somewhere drawing flies. Drawing so many flies.

He finished the bourbon and poured another. *Mr. Robot* was on the DVR. He was four episodes behind and maybe it was finally time to catch up without her, to stop waiting and just move on.

He walked into the kitchen and wondered at the cloud of flies that seemed to sprout up around his head like a corona, spinning off in every direction. He swatted at the mass but knew they would remain out of his grip. He filled his drink and sat down, queued up *Mr. Robot*. He sipped the bourbon. *Mr. Robot* was kind of a complicated show. He exited out of the DVR and clicked onto ESPN. Sports reporters were debating something about a cornerback's character. He turned up the volume and sat back in the sofa.

•

He woke up and wondered about the fruit flies. It was possible the entire kitchen would be covered with them. It was possible they would be gone entirely. He was sitting in his bed alone and hungover with Karen's books still on her nightstand. Anything was possible.

He wondered again what she had done wrong to attract so many fruit flies. A garbage can somewhere that he didn't know about? A strategically placed fuck you slice of pineapple in a remote drawer?

He thought about her things still in the drawers, the clothes and hair supplies and skin creams she had not even bothered to take with her or throw away. The lingerie, all of it, the babydolls and camis and thongs and stockings, still waiting in the bottom drawer of her vanity. He wasn't sure if he should be relieved that she hadn't packed the Very Sexy Halter Babydoll he'd bought only two months ago. $39.99 plus shipping and he'd never even seen it out of the packaging.

The coffee maker seemed normal at first, but when he opened it up a swarm of fruit flies immediately circled his head. He paused, slowed down. If he calmed down, he noticed, they calmed down.

There was one on the windowsill. It was tiny, wings and head smaller than a pencil tip. He brought his hand up slowly and brought it down hard. He looked at his palm—a tiny brown smear. He regarded the cabinets. A small brown spot. *Thwack*. With each concussion there was a flurry of movement, other flies scurrying off to safety. But if he waited, watched, he could follow one of them to the place where it alighted and then *bam*, another smear on his hand. He stalked the room, palms open like a kung fu master. He sought out the places where they gathered, the high places on the cabinets, the top of the refrigerator, the kitchen windowsill.

The coffee percolated and he thought to himself, that coffee is mine. That coffee is not yours. *Thwack. Bam*. He took them out one by one and he looked at his palms and he knew that he was making progress—he was doing it, one small brown smear at a time.

•

He put his key in the door and imagined what he was going to find—a spotless kitchen, Karen sitting at the table with a glass of wine and an apology on her face.

At first everything was the same, even the kitchen. No hovering cloud of little flies. The cabinets were still dark brown, the countertops lighter brown, the table lighter still. Maybe his morning offensive had actually worked.

But as he got closer, he saw them: tiny little dots on the cabinets, the coffee maker, the windowsill above the sink. A casual movement here and there as one buzzed from one place to another. They were ringed all along the top of the bourbon glass, a pool of them swimming in the finger of liquid at the bottom. He picked up the glass and they flew up into his face. He closed his eyes and the glass shattered. He had had a few drinks in the afternoon and he felt suddenly drunk, swaying and disconnected. There was glass on the floor, flies on every surface. He was not winning this battle.

This is exactly what she would have wanted, he thought. It was probably the reason she planted the pineapple slices in the first place.

It had been a bad day. Awful meetings, including a one-on-one with Paul for which he was unprepared and couldn't even muster the energy to bullshit. Finally Paul had just checked his email, or pretended to, and expressed his disappointment, his expectation that he "would have something to bring to the table" next week.

He found the bourbon and a new glass, poured a few fingers, and sat down in front of the television. A reporter who looked too young to be out of high school was standing in front of the hospital, the words "Flu Epidemic?" written on the bottom of the screen.

He wondered what it was that had changed. Was it Karen? The flies? When did his one-on-ones with Paul turn from a chance to show off to an embarrassment, an hour that he had to worry about his glasses fogging up, his face turning red, the scent of his breath?

A fruit fly roamed past his head and landed right in the bourbon. It was Four Roses, not the expensive one but even the middle one was more than twenty-five bucks. He looked at the fly. It was still alive, swimming desperately in the golden whiskey. That is a much better death, he thought, than however I am going out. He held the glass up toward the clouds of insects in the kitchen and downed it in one gulp.

•

He awoke in the middle of the night and had to use the bathroom. His mind registered several items: fruit flies, he had gotten too drunk, things were seriously bad at work, Karen had not come home. There was a way to deal with the fruit flies that he was not thinking of yet. There had to be.

He walked into the kitchen and to the sink, waved his hands around near the windowsill, and they flurried, roaming up around his head, behind it, above it, every direction. One of them alit on the white windowsill and he waited until it was still. He swung his hand down and *smack*. He regarded the brown smear. All around him, they flew lazy parabolas from one of their places to another, the cabinet to the top of the refrigerator, the top of the entryway to the windowsill. It was all the same, again and again.

They tended to group, to fly upwards when disturbed. They liked to sit on the windows, and he was worried that eventually he was going to put a hand through the glass, wind up in urgent care explaining the situation. Could he explain the situation?

He needed to be more gentle than the thwacks against the cabinets and the windows. He needed for his attempts to count. No more slamming a hand against the corner of the doorway only to come away with a bruise and a fruit fly drifting steadily off toward the top of the cabinet.

He went into the garage. It had not been cleaned since Karen's exit— how could he worry about something like the garage when his wife had left him, when the coffee maker was covered in tiny little flies? The garage was full, the snow blower pushing up against the mountain bikes, everywhere boxes waiting to be broken down for recycling. They expected them to be separated, the glossy not-really-cardboard from the actual-cardboard, and who could even tell, really? He pushed past a stack of newspapers and grimaced when they fell. Karen never did figure out a schedule for the recycling.

When he walked back into the kitchen, fruit flies taunted him, flying this way and that, seemingly unaware of his presence. He wrapped a length of duct tape around his left fist, did the same with his right. He flexed both hands. This might work. He advanced to the windowsill, the easiest option. There were three little brown dots sitting side by side, an inch apart. He held up both hands, moved them slowly, then slammed down on the windowsill. He held it against the plastic for a moment, and then checked the results. There, on the duct tape, three little brown dots, an inch apart.

•

He woke up and checked his phone. He had been up late last night, but there had been a real breakthrough in the fruit fly situation. He remembered opening another bottle of bourbon, wrapping himself in duct tape like a boxer heading into a fight, all those little dots on the tape.

It was late. He was supposed to be at work right now. Could he call in sick after that meeting with Paul? Maybe that was the move, actually: encroaching flu was a perfect explanation for what had been happening at work lately. He remembered the headline on the television: Flu Epidemic. The timing was perfect.

He wrapped himself in the duct tape and took stock of the situation. The same flies? The same places? Was that possible? It seemed like there were the same amount of them, more maybe, fluttering up around his head.

Soon they would be doing the scrum at work, talking about the day's projects, the week, the obstacles and opportunities. It never ended.

•

The lighter was not the most efficient solution, but when it worked it was glorious: a flame, a fly moving in the wrong direction, a quick *zap* and no more fly. There were dark marks on the windows and his right hand was wrapped in a bandage of napkins, but every time he hit one just right—*sizzle zip*—it was amazing.

The phone had been ringing. The work number and then Paul's cell. Not answering was actually smarter than answering. He was sick, in bed, too sick and too in bed to answer the phone. What was he missing? Client calls? Scrums? It was all going to be there whenever he decided to come back. He had always pushed for a two week vacation, long enough to forget about work, long enough for the two of them to find whatever it was that had gone missing, but Karen would never do it.

The television was on with the sound turned down. More people standing in front hospitals, the words "Georgia Flu Epidemic" at the bottom of the screen.

It was three in the afternoon and he probably should have had something to eat. One hundred thirty six fruit flies had been burned—*zip flash*.

He checked his phone: work, work, work, Paul, Paul.

There were lumps on his arms and his fingertips were burned. He poured more bourbon. Outside, people drove cars and rode their bikes and he couldn't imagine how they went about acting like everything was normal. A fly floated over his head. Then another. They were moving, migrating, colonizing the territory beyond the kitchen.

A knock on the door. Could that be? He froze. There it was again: knock knock knock. Then again, on the window. Then back to the door. "Come on goddamit!" a familiar voice shouted from the porch. He put down the lighter and regarded the flies. He couldn't escape the feeling that opening the door would break some kind of dream, and like Dorothy he would be swept up and brought to some other place entirely. "Wait here," he said to the flies. "This isn't over yet." The flies circled and landed, circled and landed.

He tiptoed toward the door. Through the curtains he saw his brother in law's ridiculous truck pulled up on the lawn, his brother in law's ridiculous head moving back and forth as he paced. He opened the door a crack. "What are you doing here?" he whispered.

"The fuck are you whispering?" Randall whispered back. He smelled like gasoline and smoke and whiskey. His eyes were red and he was wearing a sweatshirt with fraternity letters. There was something off with him, more off than usual even.

"What are you doing in that shirt, Randall?" he said.

"Just call me fucking Fernsler like everybody else."

"What do you want, Randall? I'm busy." He pictured the flies multiplying and stole a glance behind him. Everything looked normal, but he knew differently.

"I don't give a shit if you got a woman back there.

A man. Whatever," Randall said. "She's not even my real sister you know."

"I need to get back to what I was doing," he said, "things are...unfinished."

Randall laughed. "Think I don't know the feeling?" he said. "Jesus Christ nothing's ever fucking finished."

"So what are you doing here?"

He looked behind him and shuffled his feet. "Look. I am sorry but...anybody comes around asking I was mowing your lawn yesterday, you need to tell them yes."

"Oh, Jesus, Randall. You're not..."

Randall stepped up onto the porch. He was tall and thick and even his beard looked angry. He stepped back down onto the grass. "Look I thought I was but now I don't know." He felt the grass and then smelled his hand. "I mean I have bills and rents and Mr. Thayer on Tuesday and Reichenbach so if somebody comes around just..."

He knew what it was that was different about Randall. He was scared. Through all of it—the arrest and jail and this sad new life he had made for himself, mowing lawns and drinking beer and who knew what else, he had been so self-assured. And now he was talking about bills and meetings and who knew what else. Smelling his hands and kneeling in the lawn and asking for favors. He smelled so much like gasoline. That was it. "I will," he said. "If anybody comes. I'll tell them." He closed the door. He went into the garage. He heard Randall's ridiculous truck starting up and driving off and he had the feeling that he might never see his brother in law again.

Karen had bought the Weed Dragon years ago in an uncharacteristic fit of concern about the yard. It was a torch attached to a propane tank and she'd bought the thing with the intention of burning the weeds out of the patio brick. It hadn't worked very well and she forgot all about it and the yard soon enough, but there had been something very sexy, in a comic book kind of way, about watching his wife walk around the back yard in her work shorts, shooting flames.

The text alert buzzed on his phone. Then again, and again. He put the phone back into his pocket and brought the Weed Dragon into the house.

•

The Weed Dragon was spectacular. Before, he had been limited to one-on-one fruit fly killing, now he could eliminate an entire region of them. He could zap them straight out of thin air. Into thin air. It was beautiful.

He paused and realized he was sweating, breathing heavily. His arms felt purposefully exhausted. It felt good.

The smoke alarms had been going off for the past fifteen minutes. Or maybe an hour. It was getting dark outside. Maybe two hours. He had almost gotten used to the constant sharp beeping.

The places where they gathered, the cabinets and the windowsills and the top of the refrigerator, were scorched with burn marks, black, brown, and gray.

A fly drifted over his head and without even thinking he triggered the propane and shot a plume of flame upwards. *Zap*. The only evidence of the fly's existence was a black scorch mark the size of a basketball on the ceiling. It was amazing.

He sat down and drank from the Makers bottle. He was going to need to go to the liquor store soon but he couldn't imagine going outside.

He thought he heard the doorbell and wondered whether it was more likely to be Karen or firemen or police. He wondered if John and Mary could hear him next door, if they would call the police, if John was going to come over and tell him more bullshit stories about taking pictures in Afghanistan. He looked outside but didn't see anybody there. He wondered when he had eaten last. You could make it a week without eating, but water was another thing. There was maybe one shot left in the bourbon bottle, a few bottles of wine out in the garage, a six pack of Corona. He would be fine. He just needed to get rid of these fruit flies and everything could go back to normal. It was so obvious, a series of steps that had to be taken in the right order: take care of the flies, Karen comes home, everything goes back to normal.

He checked the propane, put some newspaper on the counters, the top of the refrigerator, filled the tops of the cabinets full of last Sunday's Times. Take care of the fruit flies, Karen comes home, everything goes back to normal. He was really looking forward to a decent sleep, a cup of coffee at the kitchen table, *SportsCenter* chattering from the living room while the *Today* show prattled on from the bedroom.

He lit the newspaper and backed up into the living room. The paper smoldered and then bloomed into flame and then the smoke was everywhere. He waved the Weed Dragon around in circles, from top to bottom, looking for stragglers coming out of the flames.

The smoke was getting thicker, a physical presence pushing him down to the floor and finally out onto the lawn. The rest of the house was starting to glow—the living room, the bedroom. The entire house was smoking.

He imagined all those tiny little bodies fizzling in the flames. The fire would find them in the places he couldn't, the backs of the cabinets, under the sink, wherever Karen had put the goddam pineapple slice that had started the whole thing. She would be surprised, he thought, that he'd taken care of things so thoroughly. Even she would have to admit that the flies were not coming back. Soon, everything would return to normal.

THE FIRES VI

Emily went out into the yard and sat in her place near the garden. The sky was black and she could barely see through the birds that circled every day now. At first they had bothered her. Dirty animals, flying in a way that seemed unnatural, evil even. Then she had started to wonder if they were the winged angels, if their constant caws and shrieks were the bellowing trumpets. Maybe the sickness hadn't been the rapture at all, but instead a cleansing. There were so few left, so many gone. If she was being honest with herself, and there was no point in hiding anything now, there being nobody else to be honest or dishonest with, these results were much closer to the tally she had been running in her head all these years. She didn't understand why Pastor McAllister would have gone in the cleansing. Or Evelyn Snyder, or Thomas Ray, or the nice little girl who used to ride her scooter past the yard and wave hello. But if the past year was proof of anything, it was that He indeed worked in mysterious ways.

Now she regarded the birds hopefully and was careful to keep her thoughts on His Word, even when making her way through their waste to her chair, wiping the scat off the arms, sitting down with the umbrella under their constant circling. She peeked out and they seemed to be massing into a spiral, whirling tighter and tighter like something from an old fashioned funhouse. "They who wait for the Lord shall renew their strength; they shall mount up with wings like eagles; they shall run and not be weary; they shall walk and not faint," she whispered.

She heard a dull roar in the distance and wondered if it was a flood. Should she have been building an ark? She had prayed on it and if she was being honest with herself, again, she hadn't really received an answer either way.

She smelled smoke in the distance. Was that sound fire? If she was really being honest, it had been some time since she had really felt His presence. Maybe the last time had been just after the sickness, when the traveling Shakespeare troupe had come through. It was so surprising, such a delight amid so much death and uncertainty and she had been able to forget, if only for an evening, the question of whether she had been preserved for rapture or left behind.

The roar was getting louder and the smoke seemed to be coming from all directions, somehow, getting closer like a beast stalking pray. She watched as small flames alit near the garden, over behind the shed, on the roof of the house. She put the umbrella down. The birds had disappeared and for the first time in the past few weeks she noticed the sky, how dead it looked now, like staring into the clear open eyes of a corpse. She had known all along that the birds were not angels. She opened the Bible and then closed it again. She put it in her lap and waited.

THE COMBAT PHOTOGRAPHER HESITATES

The combat photographer stared at the numbers on the computer. "It's not good," his wife said, indicating the row along the bottom. "I mean, what are we going to do about kindergarten?" The combat photographer looked at the numbers. A panicky feeling grew in his chest. He had no idea what this spreadsheet was supposed to show him about kindergarten, the failing public school versus the expensive private ones whose brochures littered the table.

He looked at the photos along the living room wall: Mogadishu, Chechnya, Iraq, Syria. He made the face he made when people looked at his work, and his wife made a jerking off motion with her hand. "Not the time," she said. "This is serious."

"I know. I mean...I'm a combat photographer," he said.

She sighed. "Yeah, but are you really, though, John?" The worst thing was the affection in her voice. She wasn't taking a shot across the bow, or looking to start a fight. She was trying to help him.

He looked at the back wall again. The best thing about being a combat photographer was that it was all about the work. Nobody cared what his receipts looked like when he took the photo of the little girl playing with a broken doll in the Syrian refugee camp. Nobody asked about how much he owed on the Discover Card or how many times the county had fined them for the lawn when they saw the photo of the young soldiers playing soccer while Baghdad burned in the distance. You made a picture and that was it. There was no accounting, no follow-up appointments, updating software and timetracking and bill paying and meetings, none of the exhausting maintenance of living like a regular, adult person in the world. He had no idea how other people did it. He would never be able to manage any of it without Mary.

On the table in front of them, bills and brochures, the laptop with its confounding spreadsheet, the baby monitor hissing white noise. From the neighbor's house, the sounds of something banging. *Bang bang bang*. There it was again. He wondered if he should go over there and check. "You think I should..." he said, indicating the fence that separated the two houses.

"We have our own shit to worry about," she said. "Plus," she waved at the television, where a reporter was standing in front of a hospital, what looked like a traffic jam of ambulances behind him, the words "14 Dead in Flu Epidemic" across the bottom of the screen.

Is his fire alarm going off?"

"We're not calling 911 with all of this shit going on," she said. "Not for fucking Tony and his self-inflicted quote 'problems.'"

"So this..." he pointed to the computer. "Kindergarten?"

"Okay, hear me out," she said, pointing back to the spreadsheet. The combat photographer knew he was not going to like what was coming next. "I think we should at least *think* about the house. We wouldn't get what we paid but at this point I don't think that would be the worst thing. I mean, these schools..."

More banging from next door. The houses were only sixteen feet apart, separated by a stand of bamboo and an ancient fence, and they had been able to track the progress of Karen's decampment—the fights getting worse until they receded into an eerie silence—without leaving their own kitchen table. "At least we wouldn't have to worry," she said, "about however that is going to end over there."

The combat photographer picked up a brochure. A multicultural group of kids were sitting in a circle while a beautiful young woman in dreadlocks pointed out something on an iPad. There was no price anywhere on the brochure. He had learned that this was a sign. "Sell the house?" he said. "And live where?"

"I don't know," she said. "There's only three of us. An apartment might be nice. No yard to mow. I mean, maybe we're just not house owning people. You're a combat photographer."

He looked at the numbers on the spreadsheet again, trying to make them make sense. If she was pulling out the combat photographer thing, it must be even worse than he thought.

"We could talk to my parents," she said. "Get a loan. Maybe look at moving back to Harrisburg. There's an airport there and if we didn't have to pay the mortgage on this damn house. If Tyler could just go to public school…"

The combat photographer stood up. "I'm gonna…" he said, and then he was walking, through the kitchen and out the sliding glass door and into the yard. He realized he had been sweating. Outside it was cool and crisp. He could hear traffic, a siren somewhere, the high whine of crickets, Tony still banging around next door. There was definitely a beep and he wondered again about the fire alarm. Probably Tony had forgotten to replace the battery, or he didn't know how, or he thought he was punishing

Karen by punishing himself.

The worst thing was that he knew Mary was right. Of course she was right. He had made all the sacrifices— coming out of the field, turning down the job with *Vice*, taking the job with the museum, all those hours photographing moths and rocks and bones, and it had still not been enough. They had a child, a beautiful, funny, smart child for whom he would run through the sliding glass door right now, and they couldn't even afford to send him to fucking kindergarten.

He had seen some of the most dangerous places in the world, had photographed Somali pirates and gotten drunk with Chechen rebels in Afghanistan but in the end, when all was said and done and in the only way that actually really mattered, he had been no match for stately Washington, DC, its cherry blossoms and bureaucrats and quicksand of a real estate market.

He felt for a pack of cigarettes and remembered for the thousandth time that he'd given up smoking when he'd come in out of the field. From inside, he could hear the boy crying softly and then louder, shouting for his mother. The noise was urgent and primal and it goosed a shiver up his spine.

He could hear Tony talking to himself next door. Through the fence he saw an occasional glow, or flash, and again he thought about checking to see if his neighbor was okay but Mary was right, they had enough of their own problems.

He walked past the flagstone patio they put in when they first bought the house. After a few hard hours, they had lost interest, gotten lazy and neglected to dig a foundation and lay sand, as indicated by all the home improvement books.

When the ground froze, the flagstone popped and it sat now, uneven and chipped, a jagged and dangerous toddler obstacle course. They would have to start again, pull up everything, buy new flagstone, dig the hole deep enough this time, haul sand up the hill, think about variations in rock thickness and average rainfall and drainage patterns.

This is who they would need to become, he thought—direction followers, work glove and protective eyeglass wearers, the kind of people who don't abandon plans halfway through to drink wine on some half-assed patio.

He stepped around the corner until he could see them in the bedroom, Mary holding the boy, whispering into his ear, her head pressed against Tyler's lovely, miraculous face. Pale green light from the dehumidifier bounced around the room and his little family looked like they were glowing, lit from within. He reached for the Canon and snapped a few shots before he realized even what he had done.

He heard a new sound from next door. It was familiar, somehow, but he couldn't place it—a loud rush of air, like a machine exhale—and then Tony laughing like an idiot. The suburbs. Jesus. They were practically on top of each other. Tony and Karen had seemed like good neighbors when they first moved in. They had even shared a few meals, a few beers along the fence. Since Karen had left, though, Tony seemed to have locked himself up in the house and now this…whatever this was. Mary was right: it was not going to end well.

The combat photographer sat down on the rocky little patio. The stones pushed at his bottom. He was amazed the boy hadn't already tripped and impaled himself on the damn thing. From next door, familiar flashes of light, a glow erupting suddenly into flames. He turned to see Mary shouting something at him, knocking on the window and gesturing toward the street while the flames from next door were growing ever larger in the reflection. He thought about all the things in the house, the pieces of paper that certified their marriage and Tyler's birth, the bills and checkbooks and receipts, the laptop and its spreadsheet, more revealing than any photo he would ever take. The combat photographer grabbed his camera and launched himself over the fence.

THE FIRES VII

The only reason Cutter came into the Center at all was that Mr. Bailey had asked him to, and Cutter still took pride in doing what he was asked, in doing it well and quietly and without being asked again. He hadn't yet broken the pact he had made with himself when he left Maryland. If he was going to start again, really this time, even with everything that had happened, he was going to honor the pact. And it was even more important now. In the end, after all, who was going to be left to bargain with?

He had believed in God once. A God, at least. Something. But that went away in Maryland. Today was New Mexico and the Center and the machines and the instructions from Mr. Bailey, typed and doublespaced and right where they were supposed to be in the locked file cabinet. "To be used only in the circumstance of nuclear or other apocalypse," read the title on the folder, in Mr. Bailey's neat handwriting. The most amazing thing, Cutter thought, was that Mr. Bailey had written these instructions a full four years ago, before the sickness, even. Cutter didn't know how long he had left, but he knew he'd never be the man Mr. Bailey was.

The instructions were clear. He was to lock down completely and follow the process for re-animation. The low hum of the facility, the machines and the coolers and occasional machine beep or whirr had unnerved him at first, like being in the heart of some massive sleeping robot, but over time he had come to regard their presence as a comfort. He gauged the silence now as he climbed the stairs toward the hatch. He swung the door open—a spaceship door is how he had always thought of the large half-moon cut into the desert floor—and was immediately overcome with smoke and heat. He pulled the door shut, coughing, and followed lockdown procedure as best he could with his eyes streaming tears. It was time.

He had learned to call them patients but never to really feel that way about them, like there was a real person in there who might eventually be unfrozen and come back to life whenever science was ready to facilitate a rebirth. Even with as much respect as he had for Mr. Bailey, the whole thing just seemed like a rich person's last gamble, one more way their money might be used to gain any possible advantage, even in death.

Now he went through the re-animation procedure, flicking buttons and setting temperatures, starting with the oldest patients and working his way to the most recent. The sounds had changed slightly and he wasn't sure if it was the re-animation procedures or the fire above. He wondered if liquid nitrogen was explosive. Although he knew it could take weeks, he couldn't help from watching the encasements, half expecting them to slowly open. My god, he thought, what would happen to them if somehow it all worked?

At the very end of the instructions, Mr. Bailey had hand-written a final paragraph titled "For Mr. Cutter." There, the man had outlined how Cutter was to program a chamber for one week from the current date, and then enter. "They will need somebody to help them orient," he had written. "They will need you." The old man really did believe, after all.

The room was getting hotter and Cutter was pretty sure the sound was fire roaring above. He followed instructions, finding the heavy cryo suit in the exact place Mr. Bailey said it would be, then pre-setting the lock. He settled down into the nitrogen—warm and floaty. He held his breath. He closed the door.

THE COMBAT PHOTOGRAPHER'S WIFE

The combat photographer's wife watched the police and the fire people picking through the damage. There were only a few of them. She knew from the news that most emergency personnel had been directed to the hospitals, where people were dying. Off to the side, a tall man in a suit pecked away at an iPad. A woman in rain boots and a skirt did the same on the stairs that led from the street up to the yard. Mary realized she had forgotten to turn the car off, that she was idling in the street, staring at the people working through the blackened remains of her neighbor's house—a crime scene now? Almost surely a crime scene—and she turned off the car and reminded herself to act normally.

She walked up her own stairs casually swinging the lunch bag—shit, she had forgotten to drop Tyler's lunch at daycare. She would have to wait until nap time, sneak in and leave the lunch without being seen in order to prevent any backsliding. He was having trouble with transitions, a normal problem from everything she had read, even a good one, but still, better to sneak in and out without a tantrum. Today they could not afford any more trouble.

She waved to the person who seemed to be in charge—a ruddy older man with red hair and a badge pinned to his windbreaker. "The neighbor?" he said. "Mrs…"

"Mary Holly," she said. "Yes. The neighbor."

"I'm Beeks," he said, indicating the badge clipped to his windbreaker. "You have a minute?" As he spoke, he was already folding the pages of his notebook, making a new space to write.

"I really have to..." she said.

"Truth is we're going to have to wrap this up soon and get all available people down to the hospital, so...."

"Sure," she said. "Yes. Of course. Just let me get rid of this bag." She swung the lunch bag up into his face and smiled too much and walked back to the house. She watched the ground. She couldn't see anything, at least, no stains or traces from what she could tell.

She came back out to find Beeks talking with the man and woman in the suits. "We're going to have to wait, run through the process," he said.

"With the brother in law, though?" said the woman. "And this pandemic or whatever they're calling it?"

"We find him then maybe," he said. "You know how this goes. We work through the process and we see what we see."

"Shit," the woman said. She was short, wearing expensive clothes and nice make-up. She was the kind of pretty Mary's mother would have called 'put together,' the kind of pretty she had always worked toward but never quite achieved in her time at Pfizer. "They're telling us we need to get out of the field, get home and wait out whatever this is," the woman said.

"Any chance..." Beeks said. He let the question sit in the air.

"Let me see," the woman said. She locked eyes with Mary and trudged back toward the stairs, pecking a number into her phone. Mary noticed her boots were the kind of boots she had seen the neighborhood girls wearing—rubber and colorful.

"So," Beeks said, turning his attention to Mary. "Speaking of the neighbor. I understand Mr. Lenig is in your residence right now?"

She nodded. "Asleep I think. He was…last night was, well, you can imagine. He's lost everything."

"Of course, of course," the man said. "Thing is, we have a lead on this. The brother in law, a Mr. Fernsler. Ring a bell?"

She shook her head no. Fernsler?

"Arrested for arson once already. Did a stint in Rockview. His apartment building burned a few days ago —not the whole thing, just a few units, including his, but he's been missing ever since and we have a warrant out for him as a person of interest in that case. This one, well, it does look like it could add up."

"My goodness," Mary said. She wondered if Tony was awake, if John was awake, how long they would have to play good neighbor, if she still had Karen's cell number in her phone.

"Possible to…" Beeks started.

"Sure," Mary said, before she even thought about it. She hated the chipper sound in her voice. Everybody needed something, their diapers or kitchens or checkbooks cleaned, their paperwork filed, their questions asked for them.

She walked the short space between the houses, looking down for any signs. She couldn't see anything but that didn't mean *they* couldn't. Calm down, she told herself. They didn't even seem to be looking at Tony and he was the one they found in the front yard with burns up and down his arms and a blood alcohol level of .22.

She paused in the foyer and held her trembling hands

out. She hadn't even really thought about it the night before, just grabbed the gas can and poured a line from Tony's door to their own. For just a moment it had seemed like a gift, a chance to start over without going thirty or forty thousand dollars in debt, a chance to reset, like advancing a level on a videogame—everything would be new, clean, fresh, all their old problems gone. It probably wouldn't have worked, she thought. It didn't work.

The house was trashed—dishes stacked in the sink, Tyler's clothes all over the place. John's keys were on the counter and she wondered if he had called in sick or just slept in. Sometimes, after so many years in the field, he still had trouble with the finer points of being a normal person. Sometimes she almost felt guilty about the changes in his life, but then she thought about Tyler and the guilt fizzled away.

The television was on in the living room, Tony and John sitting mute while a man in a blazer stood outside a hospital. The words "Georgia Flu: Hundreds Dead in Pandemic" were displayed at the bottom of the screen. The show went to a commercial and the men remained silent. On the television, four men were playing golf and talking about a blood thinning drug. She recognized a few of them, probably athletes. Things happened that were almost funny and then they were reciting a list of terrifying side effects and she thought again of her time at Pfizer. Another set of men wanting something, wanting for their arms to be squeezed, to watch her walk out of the office in her tight skirt, to be taken for dinners and given tchotchkes for their grandchildren.

The television switched to another commercial—this one either for a movie or a videogame, she couldn't tell any more. Tony and John remained silent, both of them under blankets in their separate chairs, coffee steaming next to them, and she almost felt guilty for being the one to break the reverie, to usher in the ending part of whatever this was, the part with Officer Beeks and people entering information into forms that would be evaluated by other people and eventually would end in...what?

"Tony," she said quietly, and then when he didn't even move, "Tony!"

He jumped and looked at her with genuine surprise. She wondered if he was that focused on the videogame commercial, if he was thinking about the house and his things and his wife long gone, or if he really was simple enough to just be sitting there thinking about nothing.

"Police outside asking for you. About the..."

"Have you, uh...have you talked to Karen at all?" he said.

She shook her head.

"I thought that..." he said.

"The officer in charge out there is named Beeks. He's the one looking for you," she said. Her voice was more sharp than she intended. She toned it down: "you better go talk to him."

Tony stood and the blanket dropped on the ground. He was wearing sweatpants and a Dave Mathews Band tee shirt. He nodded as he passed. She heard the front door open and close. She was almost certain he hadn't seen what she did last night. Even if he had, he was so drunk, so crazy, shouting about flies and Karen and everything getting back to normal. Even if he did tell Beeks what he saw, they almost certainly wouldn't believe him.

She picked up the blanket and folded it, put it back on

the chair. John looked at her expectantly. The pile of dishes sat on the kitchen counter. "Did you call in?" she said, and he turned his head like a dog hearing an unexpected noise. He coughed and looked at his hand. Blood. "You better call in and tell them you're sick," she said, fighting the panic fluttering in her chest. She handed him the phone and went into the kitchen.

THE FIRES VIII

Mary woke up and remembered all over again. They were gone. John and Tyler and everybody. The feeling was like stepping into an ice cold bath: she woke up neutral and then remembered everything, the sickness and the birds and then the fires and now...she wasn't really expecting there to be anything next. She was alive and the simple fact of it was more of a curse every day. Every night she went to sleep hoping it would be the last time. Every day she woke up and wondered why, how much longer, if the dogged sense of duty would desert her today and finally allow her to put the gun in her mouth and pull the trigger.

She sat up, unraveled herself from the tarp and took stock. The entire neighborhood—the city, the world?—was in ashes, smoking, reduced to charred rubble. The trees, houses, cars, everything. And she was alive.

The birds were gone and the silence of the dead sky was unnerving. The only sounds were the crackling and hissing of the trees, small explosions not far away that she assumed were the last of the power wires finally going. She couldn't imagine that there would again be a time when she would smell anything other than smoke. Everything was black, gray, fuming and broken. The landscape matched her own state of mind so perfectly that she wondered again if she was going mad, had gone mad, and was actually strapped into a bed in some suburban mental ward, dreaming the entire apocalypse while the rest of the world went about its day to day business.

She flashed on a memory: shopping for tilapia in Giant while Tyler stared in wonder at the lobsters. She wished her mind would stop doing this. To think that there was a time when the world was arranged in such a way that fish could be delivered across the country in a matter of days, when a toddler, her toddler, Tyler, could giggle at live lobsters bobbing in their tank, it was too much.

She stood and shouted "Hey! Hey!" Nothing. Her voice was thin and unconvincing. Did she want there to be others? What was there to even want anymore? When the birds had started circling she had taken it as a comfort—everything really had gone crazy, absurd, unreal. She wondered if the sun would be next, the moon, gravity. Each time she dropped a knife or a can of ravioli something in her was a little surprised when it didn't float into the sky and drift away.

It had all seemed so onerous, such a hassle making dinner and paying bills and shopping, changing diapers and buying band-aids and checking email, and now she knew that it had all been an incredible gift, a luxury so wonderful she couldn't even bear to think about it. Their lives had been laid out in neat and orderly rows and, like people lost in a corn maze, they had simply lacked the perspective to see it for the series of impossible miracles that it was. They had all been dreaming, and now she was awake.

When the smoke had started to overcome her, when it was clear that somehow the fires were coming from nearly all directions, she had lain down in what remained of the neighbor's house on the theory that maybe there was nothing left to burn. Even now, coughing up black phlegm, her skin and hair covered in ash, she didn't understand the will to live, why it still kicked inside her like an infant.

She walked the short distance to her own house. Nothing but charred remains of things. All of it was gone, John's photos and the baby clothes and the documents and paintings and the Kix cereal and dinosaur chicken nuggets she'd been unable to dispose of after the sickness. It was a pile, two or three feet thick, hissing and popping and smoking and that was all.

At each stage—the sickness, the birds, and now the fires—she had assumed that this was the end. When John started coughing and then throwing up, when she saw the blood easing out of Tyler's nose, she had assumed that she was next. She had even made a kind of peace with it. They would go out together, their little family like so many others, apparently, either moving on to whatever was next, or not, but doing it together. There was some comfort in that. There was no comfort in the next part, dragging the bodies down the street, pouring gas and lighting the match. There was no comfort in any of the days that followed, in the birds circling or picking through her neighbors kitchens, breaking into their gun cabinets, in the sound of the fires like a massive beast approaching from all sides.

She had seen people after the sickness, an ancient Peruvian woman who lived a few blocks away and spoke no English, the fat man who used to walk his dog around the public school. She had seen them each once and had exchanged no more than a nod before they scurried back to wherever they were staying. She had seen a few others, slipping along the back yards with backpacks or plastic bags stuffed full of canned goods or ammunition or whatever. She was past being scared of people.

She had cut a line in the soft skin above her wrist for each day after the sickness and she took out the knife, pushed it into the skin and drew line number fifteen. She watched the blood emerge almost black and then morph maroon red as it dripped down her arm. Fifteen. If this wasn't the end, then what could possibly be next?

She looked again at the rubble. There was literally nothing left.

It was a ten mile walk into the District. If there were people still alive, she imagined they would drift in that direction. She looked for something to carry but nothing remained. She went to the street and starting walking.

About the Author

Dave Housley is a founding editor of *Barrelhouse Magazine* and a co-founder and organizer of the Conversations and Connections writers' conference. He is the author of three previous short fiction collections. His work has appeared in *Hobart, Mid-American Review, Nerve,* and elsewhere.